THE WORLD OF DAUGHT[ER McGUIRE]

Sharon Dennis W[yeth]

*"Daughter—that's my name.
Daughter McGuire—I'm eleven."*

When Daughter McGuire, her mother, and her younger brothers, Satch and Jerry Lee, move next door to her grandparents, she's faced with starting over in a new school, making new friends, and keeping clear of troublemakers like the Avengers. Life would also be easier if her father hadn't run off to Colorado. If her parents were together again, her mother's creepy friend Jim Signet wouldn't be hanging around.

But things pick up when Daughter and her classmates Connie and Anna discover Topknot Cave and start the Explorers Club. And at school Mrs. Jackson, Daughter's teacher, suggests an exciting family heritage project. The hitch is that some people think that Daughter's family heritage is too "mixed-up." According to her family tree she is African-Italian-Irish-Jewish-Russian-American. One of the Avengers calls her a "zebra," because one of her parents is black and the other is white. Daughter is so upset, she begins to wonder what she *should* call herself.

As her project comes together, Daughter learns more about her background and the story of the courageous woman whose name she carries. Little does Daughter McGuire know that her own courage will soon be tested in a way she had never dreamed of.

Publication Date: April 1994
$14.95 U.S./$17.95 Can.
176 Pages
Middle Grade Fiction
ISBN: 0-385-31174-5

ATTENTION, READER:

This is an uncorrected galley proof. It is not a finished book and is not expected to look like one.

Errors in spelling, page length, format, etc., all will be corrected when the book is published several months from now.

Uncorrected proof in this form, might be called pre-publicity proof. It was invented so that you, the reader, might know months before actual publication what the author and publisher are offering.

Delacorte Press

NEW YORK

THE
WORLD
OF
DAUGHTER
McGUIRE

THE
WORLD
OF
DAUGHTER
McGUIRE

Sharon Dennis Wyeth

Delacorte  Press

Published by
Delacorte Press
Bantam Doubleday Dell Publishing Group, Inc.
1540 Broadway
New York, New York 10036

Design by Christine Swirnoff

Library of Congress Cataloging in Publication Data

Manufactured in the United States of America

April 1994

10 9 8 7 6 5 4 3 2 1

BVG

For my daughter,
Georgia Sims Wyeth,
and my mother,
Evon Dennis Bush—
who have both taught me a lot.

〰〰 1 〰〰

ONE NIGHT I locked my mother out of the house. She stood on the front porch calling, "Daughter! Daughter—let us in!"

Daughter—that's my *name*. Daughter McGuire— I'm eleven. I have a brother named Satch who's eight and another brother named Jerry Lee who's in kindergarten. My mother, two brothers, and I have just moved to a house on Cedar Street, next door to my grandparents—without my dad, Bob. Dad left and went to Colorado. The person Ma was locked out on the porch with is a guy named Jim Signet. I don't know Jim, but I'm sure I don't like him.

Ma woke me out of a sound sleep. Actually, I was having a nightmare that I was a skeleton lying in a coffin, dying of thirst. The dying-of-thirst part had to have come from the big bowl of salty popcorn Grandma Luck had made for me, Satch, and Jerry Lee just before bedtime. The skeleton-lying-in-a-coffin part probably came from the movie we'd watched on television.

I hadn't locked my mother out on purpose. The reason I'd put the night chain on the front door is that I was scared. Before I dreamed about being a skeleton, I'd been lying in bed thinking about one. The main character in the movie we'd watched had been this woman looking for treasure. At the start of the movie it was a bright sunny day. But by the middle everything was dark and the music was spooky. Instead of a treasure the woman discovered a coffin with a moldy skeleton inside of it. When she lifted the lid and screamed, Jerry Lee screamed too. And so did I, I'm ashamed to admit. Satch, who pretends never to be afraid of anything, began to laugh at us. And Grandma Luck snapped off the television.

"Told you not to put on those scary movies," she said, wagging her finger. "Up to bed." She herded us upstairs. "I promised your ma you'd be asleep by nine."

Of course I knew that didn't mean me. Satch and Jerry Lee would have to go to sleep. But I could stay up and read *Wuthering Heights*.

"Is that a kids' book?" Grandma Luck raised an eyebrow.

"I found it in a box of Dad's stuff. There's nothing dirty in it," I said, hugging the book closer.

"What's it about?" she asked.

"I'm not sure. It's fat, though."

Grandma Luck put her hands on her hips. "You've got bags under your eyes. You can read for fifteen minutes and that's it. And don't worry about your ma getting in. She took her key with her."

She bent down to kiss me. I sniffed at her neck, which smells like good almond soap. I squeezed a clump of her hair, which looks like a gray cloud. "You have cotton in your hair," I said. That's something she always says to me.

"Don't *you* be a cotton brain," she said, smoothing my greasy old bangs back.

"What are you talking about?" I said, sitting up in bed.

She squinted her eyes. "I know good and well what happened the last time you kids were in the house alone at night. You went back downstairs and turned on that television."

"That's not going to happen," I promised, remembering the skeleton. "When is Ma coming home, anyway?"

"Should be soon. She had a voter registration meeting down at the Center. Then she and that fellow she met were catching a quick bite."

"Catching a quick date, you mean," I said.

Grandma shrugged. "As far as I know, Jim's just a new friend."

"Come on, Grandma," I argued, "he likes her. He probably wants to kiss her after their date. The sad thing is, we don't know a thing about this guy—even though I can tell he's a bum."

"Your ma said he's got a business venture," Grandma reminded me.

"What kind of business venture?" I said, rolling my eyes.

"Beats me," she replied. She picked up my sneakers. "These stink. You should try putting a little talcum in them." She threw the shoes in the closet and left the room. "I'll check on Satch and Jerry Lee."

I flipped through my father's old book. I came to a part where the hand of a dead girl reaches in through a window. When my grandmother came back into the room, I jumped.

"Are they asleep?" I asked, slamming the book shut.

"Jerry Lee is, and Satch is trying. I told Satch not to turn his light back on. Anything you want to tell me?"

I shook my head and stuffed the book under the bed.

"That scary movie spooked you—didn't it?" said Grandma Luck, staring me down.

"I'm eleven years old!—not a baby, like Jerry Lee!"

"If you say so . . ." she said, tucking me into bed.

I grabbed one of her bony old fingers. "I have an idea. . . ."

"Yeah?"

"Why don't you call Grandpa Luck and have him come over? He could have leftover pizza."

"You know your grandfather hates pizza," she said, wrestling her finger away.

"How could he hate pizza?" I said, grabbing her wrist. "He was born in Italy!"

"All Italians don't have to love pizza," she sputtered. "That's like saying that everybody born in Alabama has got to love grits. Now, let me go, before you pull my arm out of the socket!"

I let her arm go and fell back into bed.

She smiled and gave me another big kiss. "Honey, you're perfectly safe. And if you need us, we're right next door. . . ."

I listened to the creak in the stairs as she hurried down them. Then I heard the front door click shut. After that I heard peepers and a car honking. I stared at my wallpaper. It's a putrid yellow with some flower in it that I don't know the name of. I thought about my old best friend, Silverine Williams. It had only been a couple of months since I'd seen her, but it seemed like two years.

Then I heard the scratching noise. It seemed to be coming from the window. I ran across the room and pulled up the shade. There was nothing outside but a full moon and darkness. I put my fingers in my ears to make the noise go away. But when I took them out again, the scratching seemed louder. My heart started pounding. Maybe there were robbers in the neighborhood. Robbers that Grandma Luck didn't know about. Or maybe the scratching came from something not human. I remembered the skeleton. Moldy —encrusted with cobwebs. Lifting itself up out of the coffin. I pulled the shade down. I really had to get hold of myself. So what if the scratching sound was now on the roof? Did skeletons climb up on roofs? Of course not. Skeletons are only found in science labs. Or in coffins. They're dead. They can't make scratching noises.

"Hey, Daughter!" Satch whispered across the hall. I jerked, then noticed his light.

"You scared me half to death," I said, rushing in. "You're supposed to be asleep." I clicked off his lamp.

"Who are you—boss of the world?" he said. He was sitting up in bed, surrounded by baseball cards. Moonlight filtered in from the street. Jerry Lee stirred in the next bed. His face was pressed against his bear and he'd thrown his quilt off.

"Shh!" I picked up the quilt. "Do you want to wake him? What do you want, anyway?"

"I just wondered if I could borrow your Roberto Clemente," he said, scooping up the cards and putting them into a shoe box.

"Knowing you, you already borrowed it."

He gave me a big grin, flashing his broken front tooth. "You know me, all right."

"Take good care of it," I warned. "Don't leave it in that box. Put it in an album. Dad gave me that Roberto Clemente."

"Forget it, then," said Satch, shoving the shoe box aside. "I don't want it, if Dad gave it to you."

We were quiet for a minute. I sat down on the edge of his bed. "Scary movie tonight, huh?" I said finally.

He shrugged. "I wasn't scared."

I got up to leave. "Me either."

Satch grabbed my elbow. "Do you think this neighborhood has drug dealers?" he asked.

"Don't be silly," I said. I cracked my knuckles. "Ma wouldn't move us into a neighborhood where there are drug dealers. Go to sleep, now. Ma will be home."

"If I was in that cool car of Jim Signet's," Satch said, settling back, "I'd stay out forever."

"His car looks like an old hearse," I snapped.

"It's a Cadillac," Satch argued, "even if it is old."

I looked out the window. "I liked our car."

"The Chevy?" said Satch.

"No, the Rabbit," I said, remembering our red station wagon, "the one that Dad took. I miss it. I miss Dad too," I said.

"I don't," said Satch. "Why should I? He doesn't miss me, does he?"

"Sure he does," I said. "He'll be back from Colorado in no time."

"So what if he does come back?" said Satch. "He and Ma are probably getting divorced."

"It hasn't happened yet," I said.

I stood there cracking my knuckles again.

"Don't do that," he told me.

"Don't do what?"

"Don't crack your knuckles," he said. "Dad is the one who always used to tell you not to," he reminded me. "Remember?"

I peered at him in the dark. His head was sticking straight up out of his covers. He reminded me of a cute little prairie dog. "I remember," I said, leaving the room.

I stood in the hall next to the bathroom. The

scratching noise was still on the roof. I listened for what felt like hours. I listened so hard that I heard my own breathing. Then I held my breath and heard my own hearing. No doubt about it, there *was* a *scratching* on the roof. It either came from a tree, a robber, a skeleton, or the hand of a ghost. Not wanting to take any chances, I ran downstairs and put on the night chain. Then I ran back up, dived into my bed, and fell sound asleep. By the time I figured out that Ma's voice wasn't part of my skeleton dream, she and Jim Signet were breaking in the living-room window.

"I've got the screen off," I heard Jim's voice say.

I crept a quarter of the way down the stairs. When I caught sight of Jim's bald head popping through the living-room window, I crouched by the banister.

"I'll climb in and take the chain off the door," I heard Ma say. Jim's shiny head disappeared. Then Ma poked her head in. My mother is beautiful. She wears her long, dark hair loose. And her brown skin hasn't got a single wrinkle. That night she was wearing her new green pants suit. She climbed through the window and walked to the front door. She undid the chain and let Jim Signet inside. She took off her green jacket.

The first thing Jim did was put on his hat. His hat

9

is big and black and covers his eyes. He had on a neon-blue suit and gold tie. After he put on his hat, he lit up a cigarette.

"Wonder what happened to Daughter," Ma said, shutting the door behind Jim. I tried to make myself smaller.

"Your daughter's dead to the world, Tess." Most people don't call my mother Tess. Most people call her Teresa.

He draped an arm around her and blew out some smoke. Ma coughed a little. "This, uh, has been, uh, quite a splendid evening," he said.

"I've enjoyed it too," Ma said, wiggling away to pick a piece of popcorn off the floor.

"You've got a great place," he said. "I dig the decor. You're so lucky to have those three little squirrels waiting here for you."

"You mean the kids?" Ma said with a laugh.

"Forgive my language," Jim said, sneaking his arm around her again. He was wearing huge, fake diamond cuff links that my father wouldn't be caught dead wearing.

I stood up and cleared my throat loudly.

Jim jumped and stared at me. I stared back at him.

"Did we wake you?" Ma asked, taking a few steps toward the staircase. "Somebody put the night chain on by mistake, so even though I had my key I couldn't get in. I climbed in through the window."

I stood there tongue-tied. Then I remembered I was wearing only my T-shirt and underwear. "I'm asleep," I announced, walking up the stairs.

"How about that?" I heard Jim say, with a whistle. "A real genuine sleepwalker."

I stopped for a drink in the bathroom, then crawled into bed. I hid my face under the covers. A couple of minutes more and Ma was out in my hall.

"Hi, sweetheart. . . ." she whispered.

I lay still and kept my eyes shut.

"Sorry I was out so late," she said. "The voter registration drive was very successful. Is everything all right here?"

I wanted to say, *No, everything is not all right here. I miss the purple roses on the wallpaper in my old room. Your date has an ugly bald head and a silly vocabulary. There's this pain in my heart, where I miss Dad.*

But I didn't say anything. I just played possum.

2

MY NEW school is called Lucy Newton Elementary.
Some people call it Lucy Fig Newton. It's up a long
hill. Across the street from the school is a church
with woods behind it. Lucy Fig Newton is brick and
hard as a rock. Everybody makes you sit up straight
there. There's no fiddling with pencils. But I don't
mind, because I'm in Mrs. Jackson's class.

Connie Boggs is in Mrs. Jackson's class too. Every
day I see the back of Connie's head, since she sits in
front of me. Every day Connie has on another big,
colorful bow. And every day before and after class
Connie turns around and smiles at me. But the first
time we really got to talking to one another was outside on the school steps. I was waiting for Satch.
Connie had her best friend, Anna Otake, with her.

"You live down Cedar Street way, don't you?" said
Connie. She has really deep dimples in her cheeks.

"Yep," I answered. "I live on Cedar Street."

Anna rocked back and forth on her feet. "Let's go," she said to Connie. "What are we waiting for?"

"In a minute," said Connie. She smiled at me a second time. "We know a shortcut. Want to walk home with us?"

I really did want to. I hadn't made any friends at Lucy Fig Newton yet. I looked at the door. Lots of kids were coming out, but not my brother.

"I have to wait for Satch," I said.

Anna made a face. "What kind of name is that? Satch?"

I shrugged.

"Come to think of it," said Anna, staring down at the hole in my jeans, "what kind of name is Daughter?"

"It's a family name," I said, feeling my neck get hot. "I'm not sure where my parents got it."

Connie sat down on the stairs. "My grandmother lives on Cedar Street too," she said, changing the subject.

I sat down next to her. "No kidding."

"What's the big deal?" Anna said, popping her gum. "You're going home with me after school. Not to your grandmother's."

Suddenly, I felt someone's toe in my back. I turned around. A tall boy with a pimply face was standing above me.

13

"Out of the way, doofus," he said. "You're sitting on my tail." Connie scooted away. "What are you talking about?" I asked.

"Just get up," the boy snarled.

I jumped up and he pointed to the stairs. There was a painting of a red insect with a long tail where I'd been sitting.

"People move when the Avengers come around," he said.

A can of spray paint was sticking out of his pocket and he was carrying a basketball. Three boys were standing behind him. One of them, whose name is Arthur Cheever, I knew from class.

"Got anything to say about it?" the pimple said, leaning into Anna's face.

Anna backed away. "Not really," she said.

One of the boy's friends began giggling—a shrimpy-looking boy with long blond hair in his eyes.

"Shut up, turkey," the pimple said, slamming the ball into the boy's stomach. "Who told you to laugh?"

Pimple started down the stairs, with Arthur and the others following him. The fourth guy was tall, too, and skinny as a string bean.

"Who are they?" I whispered.

"The Avengers," Anna replied, huddling up to me. "They walk around trying to act bad."

"The pimply one is Luke Dangerfield," whispered Connie, pointing over her shoulder. "He's their leader. Pointy-headed Arthur Cheever you already know."

"I never thought Arthur was a tough guy," I said. "In class he's such a goof-off."

"They mess things up with spray paint," Connie added. "That's Luke's mark on the stairs."

I peered down at the splotch of paint on the stairs. It looked like a red scorpion. Then I turned to watch the group of boys horsing around on the sidewalk.

"Who are the other two?" I asked.

"The shrimp is Joey Reid," said Anna. "The skinny one they call String Bean."

"They're bad news," said Connie. The boys headed down the street in a big glob. "Stay away from them."

"I'll make it a point," I said.

Satch came out of the door, swinging a violin case.

"What kept you so long?" I said, turning toward him.

"I was in the music room," Satch said. He ran

down the stairs. "Come on. Let's go to the pickle store."

"Wait," I said, running after him. "We're not going to the pickle store. We're going to take a shortcut."

Satch stopped and stuck out his chin. "I don't know about you. But I'm getting a sour pickle today."

I pointed back at Connie and Anna. "They asked us to go with them. Please . . ."

Anna came up and tapped Satch on the head. "Want to take a shortcut, Shorty?"

"No, thanks," said Satch. "And I'm not short for my age."

"So much for all our waiting around," said Anna as she and Connie started for the corner.

I yanked Satch's sleeve. "Can't you do something I want to do for once?"

"Go ahead," Satch said. "Nobody's stopping you." He walked with me to the corner and we crossed at the light. Connie and Anna had crossed too. They had started up the driveway next to the church.

"Coming?" Connie called out.

I clamped Satch on the shoulder. I tapped my foot on the ground. "Are you sure you can get home by yourself?"

"Of course I can. I'm eight."

"Make sure to wait for the lights," I warned.

He grinned and slapped my hand. "Catch you later, sis."

I ran toward Connie and Anna. They had reached the top of the driveway. They were standing at the edge of some woods. Satch ran in the opposite direction, down Morris Road.

"Isn't he a little old for baby-sitting?" Anna said as I caught up to her and Connie.

"He doesn't watch where he's going," I explained. "A few weeks ago he fell crossing the street and broke his tooth off."

"Ouch," said Connie.

We walked past the church and into the trees. "Are we going to get in trouble for trespassing?" I asked.

"Nobody cares," Connie said.

I followed them along a sunny path. The leaves on the trees were turning brown and yellow. The church was behind us. "Where does this shortcut go?" I asked Anna.

Anna shrugged. "Anywhere you want it to."

Connie turned around and walked backward. "It ends up at Pitts Place. But there's a rock where you can see the whole city."

She took a right at the fork. She led us along a path that wound uphill. A few yards away there was a flat lookout rock. The three of us got up on top of it.

"See," Connie said. In the distance I saw buildings.

"Is it the whole city?" I asked.

"Only part of it," said Connie.

"I wish we could see the whole world from here," I said.

Anna peered into the trees to our left. "Wonder what's over that way," she said.

"I'm not going to find out," said Connie. "The woods are too thick."

Anna jumped to the ground. "I'll check it out. You two go around the regular way."

Connie and I climbed down to the path again. Anna disappeared into the trees. As we walked along the path, we could hear her crashing on the other side.

"How is it in there?" Connie called out.

"Full of brambles!" Anna's shout came back. "I'll circle out and meet you."

Connie and I jogged. The sun filtered through the trees, making leaf patterns.

"She's not going to get lost, is she?" I said.

"Not Anna," said Connie.

"Well, I'm lost. I haven't the slightest idea where I am."

Connie laughed. "Don't worry. The path takes us

to Pitts Place. You can get to Cedar Street easy from there."

A few yards up we stopped.

"Anna should be coming out here," Connie said. She looked ahead and then behind her. Everything was quiet.

Suddenly, a bloodcurdling shriek filled the air. Connie and I screamed and grabbed hands. Anna leapt out in front of us.

"Gotcha!" Anna said.

"That's not funny!" Connie said.

"I thought you'd been murdered," I said, catching my breath.

"Don't be stupid," said Anna, running into the woods again. "Come and see what I found in here!"

We ran after her, pushing branches aside. Brambles stuck to my sweater and jeans. But after a few minutes the woods thinned out. There in the middle of a clearing was a stack of huge boulders with a round rock on top. The boulder on the bottom had a big hole in it.

"Wow," I said, brushing my bangs out of my face. "A cave. . . ."

"Isn't it neat?" Anna exclaimed.

We peeked into the front entrance. It was dark. Then we walked around to the back. There was a second entrance, blocked up with leaves. I ran my hand along the side of the boulder. "Nice place," I said.

Anna pointed to the small rock perched on the roof. "That little rock is cute. It's like a topknot."

"That's what we should call it," I said. "Topknot Cave."

Connie picked up a big stick and walked to the front entrance. "I hereby claim this cave for the Explorers Club!" she announced. "From this day it is called Topknot Cave!"

"What's the Explorers Club?" I asked.

"It was supposed to be a secret," Anna said, plopping down onto the ground.

"We explore places after school," Connie explained with a grin, "instead of going home and doing homework."

"Sounds neat," I said. "What do I have to do to be a member?"

Anna jabbed my foot with a stick. "Go check out the cave."

I looked at the dark hole in the boulder. "You've got to be joking," I said.

"Are you a chicken or an Explorer?" said Anna.

I looked at Connie.

"Maybe you could just peek inside for us," she suggested.

"I already did," I said.

Anna gave me another poke. "Peek in a little farther this time. We want to make sure there aren't any bears or dead bodies in there."

I got down on my knees in front of the cave. I wished I hadn't asked to be an Explorer. I reached my hand inside. The ground was moist. I stuck my head in and sniffed. It smelled like pine needles. I stuck my head in a little bit farther. A crack of light came through the back entrance. I thought of what Anna had said about dead bodies. A cave was a perfect hiding place for a corpse. I jerked myself out again, hitting my head on the rock.

"Is it scary?" Connie asked.

"Not really," I lied, rubbing my head. "I think we could unstop the back door, if we wanted to."

"Great," said Anna. "We can have our meetings in there."

I shivered. "In there? It's too dark in there."

"Maybe next time we should bring a flashlight," said Connie.

"Well, I'm not afraid," Anna said, crawling inside the cave.

Connie and I looked at each other.

"Come on in," Anna called out. "The weather's fine."

Connie crawled in first and I followed her. My heart was beating fast. I didn't like dark places.

There was just enough room for us to sit in a circle with our knees touching. In the dim light I could make out Connie smiling.

"Actually, it's kind of cozy," she said.

"So what are we going to talk about?" I said in a loud voice. I didn't want Anna and Connie to know how nervous I was.

Anna chuckled. "We each have to confess something about ourselves," she said, "something evil that we did."

"All right," Connie said. "I confess that once when I was on the roller coaster with my cousin, I laughed so hard that I wet myself. Then I hid my wet jeans from my mother and told her I'd lost them."

"That's a good one," said Anna. She looked at me. "Go ahead. Your turn."

My mind drew a blank. "I can't think of anything."

"I guess you're perfect," said Anna.

"I didn't say that," I said.

"I'll go, then," Anna said. "I confess that last summer at camp, I hated a girl so much that I put a dead frog in her pillowcase."

"Where did you get a dead frog?" I asked.

"I killed it," said Anna.

Connie screwed up her face. "You didn't."

"Okay, so it was dead when I found it," Anna admitted. "Anyway, I did put it in this girl's pillowcase. She woke up and her bed was covered with frog guts."

"Gross!" I said.

"Well, she deserved it," said Anna, "after what she did to me."

"What did she do?" Connie asked.

"First she put her fingers at the sides of her eyes," Anna said. She demonstrated, by stretching the far sides of her eyes out. "Then she started running around in circles saying stuff like 'Ah-so, chin, chong, ching,' and all these nonsense noises. She did it whenever she saw me coming."

"Why did she do that?" I asked.

"She was trying to make fun of Anna," said Connie, "because she's Asian-American."

I turned to Anna. "Are you Chinese?"

"Japanese," Anna said. "Two different countries."

"Sorry," I said.

"Lots of people were watching," Anna continued, "and they all laughed."

"You must have felt awful," I said.

"I did. What are you, anyway?"

"Come again?" I said.

"Yes, what are you?" Connie repeated, touching my shirtsleeve. "Your brother's got brown skin and you look white."

"I look like my father," I explained. "Satch looks like my mother."

Anna leaned in closer. "So what does that make you?"

"My grandma Luck is African-American. My grandpa Luck is Italian. My father's father was Irish and he's dead. And my grandma McGuire, who's alive, is Jewish," I rattled off.

"She's a mixed-up," said Anna.

Connie nodded. "She's a nothing."

Tears of anger sprang to my eyes. "Don't call me names."

"Sorry," said Connie. "We didn't mean anything by it."

"Don't be so sensitive," said Anna.

"Can we please stop talking about it?" I said, twisting away from them. My legs throbbed as I crawled toward the entrance. I'd been sitting for so long, they had fallen asleep. "Just show me the short-cut. . . ."

ഗ‍ഗ‍ഗ

Instead of Grandma Luck, who usually waits for us, Ma was out on the porch. Jerry Lee was hanging on to her leg and she had on her apron.

"Hi, Daughter," Jerry Lee said in his babyish voice.

Ma stroked my head. "Where have you been?"

"I met some friends," I answered. "This girl named Connie has a grandmother who—"

"Where's Satch?" Ma interrupted.

I looked around. Luckily, Satch was coming down the street. "There he is," I pointed out to her. "Anyway, this girl's grandmother might know Grandma—"

Ma sniffed the air. "I'm burning the rice."

"This girl's name is Connie Boggs," I said. "Do you know a Boggs?"

"Who?" Ma said, opening the door. "I don't think—" She took Jerry Lee by the hand and waved at Satch. "Hurry inside now," she called out. "After dinner I have to go back to work. There's a drug rehab meeting down at the Center." She gave me a quick smile. "Talk to me later, sweetheart."

The screen door banged shut. Satch climbed up the stairs.

"Where have you been?" I asked him.

He put down his violin and stuck his hand under

my nose. It smelled like pickle juice. It was also covered with globs of blue ink. "What's that on your hand? A tattoo?"

"It's a drawing of a spider," Satch said, proudly. "Arthur Cheever did it."

"What are you doing hanging around with Arthur Cheever?" I asked in surprise.

"He's in your class," said Satch. "He told me that he thinks you're smart."

"He's an Avenger," I said, feeling my face get hot.

"He asked me when your birthday is," Satch continued. "I think he might like you."

"Don't be ridiculous," I said. I wagged my finger at him. "The Avengers are bullies."

"Arthur isn't," he said.

"Don't hang out with him," I insisted.

"Don't you tell me what to do," said Satch, letting the door bang shut a second time.

After dinner my grandparents came over. Satch practiced his violin in the living room, while Jerry Lee and Grandma Luck listened. Grandpa Luck sat in the kitchen, while I did the dishes.

"The boy will make a good musician someday," Grandpa said, leaning his chair toward the door.

I turned to the sink. To me Satch's playing sounded like screeching.

"Penny for your thoughts," Grandpa said, jingling some coins in his pocket.

"I was thinking about exploring," I said.

Grandpa's eyes twinkled. "Anything else?"

I plunged my hands into the suds. "What would you do if someone called you a 'mixed-up'?"

"I'd probably laugh," said Grandpa.

"How about if someone called you a 'nothing'?"

He shook his head. "I wouldn't believe them."

"Okay, I won't either," I said.

He tugged my braid and put a penny in my pocket.

3

EVERY SATURDAY night Grandma and Grandpa Luck have franks and beans for dinner. My whole family loves franks and beans.

"Here come the permanent dinner guests," Grandpa Luck announced as we tried to get through the front door all at once. "Get the trough out, Millie!"

"Oink! Oink!" Satch said, falling over my feet.

"Ouch!" I said.

Grandpa tweaked my nose. "How's my favorite snout face today?"

"Okay," I said, tapping his fat stomach.

"Don't all stand in the doorway," he said, picking Jerry Lee up.

Ma put an arm around Grandpa's shoulder. "Thanks for having us again. You can smell the beans a block away."

"Who cooked them this week?" Satch asked, tossing his coat on a chair. "I hope it was Grandma."

Grandpa put Jerry Lee down and caught Satch by the stomach. "Got something against my beans, buddy?"

"No, just . . . too . . . much hot stuff!" he squealed, trying to wriggle away.

"I like Grandpa's beans," I said.

"Good for you, Daughter," Grandpa said. "My beans have magic sauce in them. Now, your grandmother's beans—"

"I heard that, Vincent," Grandma called from the kitchen.

Ma laughed. "You're both good cooks. I am kind of glad that Mother is doing the cooking tonight, though." She hung Satch's and Jerry Lee's coats on the rack. "I think Jim's taste runs on the bland side."

"Jim who?" I asked.

"Jim Signet," said Ma.

"He's coming over for dinner," Grandma reported, appearing in the kitchen doorway.

"Oh, brother," I muttered.

"Of course if I had known earlier, we would have had a company dinner," Grandma continued.

"Don't worry, Mother," said Ma. "Jim is just ordinary."

"Ordinary, my eye," I mumbled sarcastically.

Grandpa had begun tickling Satch. My brother was screaming with laughter and rolling around on the floor.

"Tickle me too!" Jerry Lee cried, pulling on Grandpa's arm.

"I can't hear myself think, Vincent," Grandma shouted over the noise. "The living room is entirely too small for that roughhouse!"

Everything got quiet.

"Come on, hogs," Grandpa whispered, hoisting Satch up off the floor. "Let's go down to the basement, where the real action is."

"Can we play with Rasputin?" Jerry Lee whispered, trotting toward the staircase.

"Sure," Grandpa answered. "Rasputin doesn't mind a little noise."

Grandma rolled her eyes as they filed past. "He'll never grow up," she said. Then she and Ma disappeared into the kitchen. In a minute or two Ma came back with a big stack of plates.

"Come help me set the table," she called out.

I was taking my time hanging up my coat. "No, thanks."

"Want to go downstairs with Grandpa and the boys?"

I sat on the arm of the couch. "Nope."

"Well, come in here and help me, then," she said.

I went into the dining room. There was a bunch of paper napkins in the middle of the table. I began to fold them into triangles.

"You look glum," she said.

"I just wish we weren't having company," I said.

"I think it'll be nice for a change."

"Well, then, I just wish it weren't Jim Signet." I creased a napkin so hard that it tore.

"What have you got against him?" Ma asked. I watched her take the bowl of artificial grapes and bananas off the table and put the salt and pepper on.

"Everything," I answered.

Ma pointed to the sideboard. "Please get out some forks."

I opened the drawer and counted out six.

"Make that seven," she said, watching me closely.

"Maybe I'll eat in the kitchen," I said. "There are only six chairs at the dining table, anyway."

"I can put in an extra one," Ma offered.

"I wouldn't mind eating in the kitchen by myself," I insisted. "Honest."

Ma marched into the kitchen and came out with an extra chair. She wedged it at the back of the table, next to the window.

"That fixes that," she said.

31

"You'll be sorry," I warned her. "I'm sure he's not the type who likes franks and beans."

Ma smiled the smile she uses when she's trying to be patient. "I think it's more the company he's after. When he called and said he was all by himself this evening . . . I felt so sorry for him."

"You mean he invited himself over?" I sputtered.

"Something like that. He likes kids."

"Fat chance," I said. "I bet he doesn't know the first thing about kids."

"Well, this will be your golden opportunity to find out, won't it?" She went down to the basement, leaving me alone in the dining room. I passed out the napkins. The knocker clacked at the front door.

"Get that, please, Daughter," Grandma Luck's voice sang out.

Jim's big black hat was pulled down to his eyebrows. He was wearing a shiny chocolate-brown suit. And his tie had the biggest yellow bird on it I'd ever seen. I looked at it and a giggle leapt out of my mouth.

"Hello there, Daughter," he said, nodding his head up and down.

I giggled some more. I tried to stop myself. But I couldn't. "I, ha-ha, hello, I, ha-ha, never saw a tie with a bird like that." I covered my mouth and ran into the living room, almost bumping into Ma.

"Come on in, Jim," she said, giving me a look. "It seems that Daughter has gotten a case of the giggles."

Grandpa Luck and the boys were coming out of the basement. Ma introduced Grandpa to Jim. I curled up on the couch and kept on laughing.

"What's so funny?" Satch said, coming over.

"Nothing." I choked, barely getting the word out. I pointed at Jim's tie.

"I think it's funny too," Jerry Lee said, not knowing what was funny, but laughing anyway.

Ma shook my shoulder. "Stop it this instant."

"Sorry," I said, finally managing to push down my laughter. I sat up straighter. I was in a much better mood than I'd been in before. "Sorry, Jim," I said. "Something struck my funnybone."

"What was it?" Grandma Luck asked, peering at me over Ma's shoulder.

"Jim's tie," I announced. Everyone stared at him. "It's so gay, it made me feel like laughing."

"Ha-ha," Satch said, "I see what you mean."

"Well, I don't," Ma said firmly. She gave Jim an apologetic look. "It's been a long week. The kids are kind of hysterical."

"Not at all," Jim said. "I like squirrels with a sense of humor." He took off his hat and put it in front of his tie. "I can take a joke. Uh, once in a while, anyway."

Everybody was quiet for a moment. "Since you're wearing a bird, you must like them," said Grandpa. "Maybe you want to meet the bird I've got down the basement."

"Uh, that's okay," said Jim.

Grandma gave Grandpa a nudge. "Jim doesn't want to be dragged down into that basement. Besides, dinner's going to be on soon anyhow." She smoothed her apron. "Just franks and beans. If I had known . . ."

Grandpa patted Jim's arm. "Don't go anywhere," he said.

Grandma went into the kitchen and Ma pointed to the armchair. "Won't you sit down?" Ma asked.

Jim sat down and took out a pack of cigarettes.

"My grandmother says that smoking is a dirty habit," I said loudly.

"Right," Jim said, stuffing the cigarettes back.

"You can smoke out on the porch," Ma offered.

"I'll go out with you," Satch said. "And after your smoke, you can give me a ride in your Cadillac."

"Don't be impolite," Ma said to Satch.

"It's copacetic, Tess," Jim said with a lopsided grin. "I'll take the kid on a ride anytime."

"Me too!" Jerry Lee said, bouncing in his chair.

I frowned. My two brothers may have been taken in by Jim and his big car, but I wasn't.

Grandpa Luck came back upstairs with Rasputin, his green parrot, on his shoulder.

"Hello," the parrot croaked. "Are you a pretty boy?"

Jim jerked in his chair. "Did that thing talk?"

"Yes," Grandpa said, coming closer. "He's very intelligent."

Rasputin squawked. "Hey, baby!"

Jim pressed his back into his chair. "Nice birdie," he said.

"Are you a pretty boy?" Rasputin said again.

"He's like a broken record," Jim muttered. I noticed Jim take his handkerchief out and wipe his forehead.

"His vocabulary is kind of limited," Grandpa explained, leaning closer to Jim. "But we're working on it."

"That's close enough!" Jim said, waving his hands in front of his face.

Rasputin screeched and fanned his feathers. Jim jumped up.

"What's the matter, Jim?" I called. "Don't you like animals?"

"He's really quite friendly," Grandpa insisted.

"I have a thing about animals with wings," Jim said in a raspy voice. He backed up toward the dining room.

35

"Don't worry," I said, with a big smile on my face. "He won't pluck your eyes out."

Jim began to breathe hard. "Will you please get that chicken out of my face!" he exploded.

"Well, if you put it that way," Grandpa said, turning around in a huff. "You're obviously not a bird man," he said, making his way to the basement.

"I got a thing about wings fluttering in my face," Jim said, once Grandpa had left. He was still breathing hard. I smothered a giggle and Ma gave me a look.

"I'm so sorry," Ma said, coming over. "Pa just dotes on that parrot of his. Sometimes I think he likes him more than he likes people."

I grinned. Jim Signet had made a big mistake. Now Grandpa Luck would be on my side.

"Dinner is served," Grandma Luck said, coming out of the kitchen.

A big platter of franks was in the middle of the dining-room table and next to it a huge bowl of baked beans. Then there was a platter of homemade rolls and a bowl of cole slaw, some green salad, mustard, relish, and pickles. Glasses of milk were at the kids' places and the grown-ups had iced tea. I was hurrying to get the seat wedged in by the window, when Grandma nabbed me.

"You sit next to Jim," she said. "Jerry Lee can squeeze in back there by the window."

"But—" I caught Ma's eye. "Sure," I said, taking the chair next to Jim's. "I'd love to."

"This is some good chow," Jim said, reaching for a roll.

Jerry Lee nudged him. "We have to say grace."

"Right," Jim said, letting the roll drop.

Grandpa said the blessing, then clanged on his glass. "Hear ye, hear ye! This gathering of the hogs can now come to order!"

"Oh, gosh." Ma sighed. "Not the hogs, tonight."

"I'm the frank hog!" Satch cried, jumping up in his chair.

"I'm the bean hog!" I yelled.

"No, I'm the bean hog!" said Jerry Lee.

"We'll flip for it," Grandpa said, reaching for a roll off the platter.

"Now, Vincent . . ." warned Grandma.

"Nonsense, Millie," said Grandpa, tossing the roll in the air.

"Heads!" I cried.

"Tails," said Jerry Lee.

"Saturday night wouldn't be Saturday night without the Hog Club," said Grandpa, catching the bread. "Sorry, Jerry Lee. It's heads. Why don't you be the bread hog? Bread's very important, the staff of life."

Jerry Lee lifted an eyebrow. "Does it taste good?"

"Delish," Grandpa said, taking a bite.

"That settles it," said Satch. He forked a frank onto his plate, while I served myself beans. Grandpa gave Jerry Lee a big buttered roll.

"All right, hogs," Grandpa said. Jerry Lee put the roll to his lips and Satch and I picked up our forks. "Let's chow down!"

We gobbled up our food as fast as we could. Grandpa clanged his glass with his knife. "All right! Round one!"

Everybody stopped eating to see how we had done.

"I almost finished my hot dog," Satch announced.

"I finished my bread," Jerry Lee muttered with his mouth full.

I held up my plate. "All gone," I said.

"Good hogs," said Grandpa. "Now let's go to the second round."

"Your pop is some jive cat," I heard Jim to say to Ma. "What's all this hog stuff? Some new thing?"

Ma looked embarrassed. "It's a game Pa thought up to help the kids with their appetites," she explained.

"Doesn't seem as if they need help anymore," Jim said, looking around at us.

"I think we'd better call the Hog Club quits for a

minute," Grandma said to Grandpa, "at least until our guest is served."

"Hey, I don't mind," Jim said. "You guys can oink-oink all you want. Though I wouldn't mind a smattering of those beans."

"Of course," said Ma, passing the bean platter. "Help yourself, Jim."

"Hey, I've got an idea," I said. "Why doesn't Jim become a member of the Hog Club?"

"Yeah, why not?" said Satch.

"I don't think so," Ma jumped in.

"Why not?" I insisted. I looked at Jim. "Of course, if you think playing with kids is a waste of time . . ."

"Who me?" said Jim. "Nothing I like better than having a few laughs with you squirrels. Sure, I'll be an oink-oink."

Jerry Lee clapped his hands and laughed.

Grandpa smiled. "You're a good sport, Jim."

I pulled over the bean platter. "Be a bean hog," I said to Jim, scooping mounds and mounds of beans onto his plate. "We'll both be bean hogs."

"And the rest of you eat something of everything," Grandma instructed.

"Hey," I said. "I've got another idea."

"What's that?" Jim asked.

"Why don't the two bean hogs have a race?"

"What kind of race?" said Satch.

"Jim and I will each have a plate of beans and the one who finishes first is the winner."

"The number-one bean hog," Grandpa said, going along with my idea.

Jim threw up his hands. "I'm copacetic," he said.

"Copa—what?" said Grandma.

"He means that it's fine with him," Ma translated.

I served myself some more beans and then loaded more onto Jim's plate.

"Whoa," said Jim. "I don't think my stomach can hold that much."

"Sure it can," I said, "especially when I put the magic sauce on."

He cocked his head. "Magic sauce?"

I reached for the little red bottle in front of Grandpa's place.

"That's very spicy," Ma warned.

Grandpa gave me a sly look. "Though it is good for digestion."

Jim pointed to his beans. "Pour it on."

"Are you sure?" I said.

He nodded.

"I'll put some on mine too," I said, pretending to be fair.

For every drop of "magic sauce" I put on my beans, I put about five on Jim's.

"I think that's enough," Jim said, mopping his brow.

"You don't have to do this if you don't want to," Ma said.

Jim winked. "If she can do it, I can do it."

Grandpa clanged his glass with his fork. "Begin!"

One bite of beans and my mouth almost exploded. But Jim's beans had to have been even hotter.

"Aiiee!" he screamed, after taking a big mouthful. "Aiiee!" Beans flew everywhere. On his bird tie, on his shirt, on Grandma Luck's tablecloth. He jumped up from his seat, covering his mouth. Ma tried to help him with a glass of water and the chair fell over. Everyone was shouting all at once and Jim had his napkin over his face. He was coughing and clutching his chest. For a minute I thought he might be having a heart attack. I was amazed at all the commotion. All I'd wanted to do was give him a little burn on the mouth.

"Why don't you walk around outside for a minute?" Grandpa had him by the arm and was leading him out of the dining room.

"I'll get some ice!" Grandma screamed, running into the kitchen.

"My mouth!" Jim groaned. "My mouth! There are third-degree burns in it!"

"Maybe we should call a doctor," Ma said.

41

"Maybe your tongue needs a Band-Aid," said Jerry Lee.

Everyone but me followed Jim out onto the front porch. I sat there drinking my water.

After a while Ma came back in. Her mouth was one thin line. "I hope you're satisfied."

I gave her a guilty look. "How did I know he was allergic to hot sauce?"

"Anybody would have burned their tongue with the amount that you put on his food," she said.

"He said he wanted to be bean hog," I argued. "He said he wanted magic sauce."

Ma tapped her foot. "I think you'd better go home."

"Before dessert?"

She nodded.

"But Grandpa is making banana splits," I protested.

Ma pointed to the back door.

I got my coat. "I don't know why it's my fault. My mouth got burned too. You didn't see me carrying on like that."

Ma put a hand on my shoulder. "It's not like you to be rude to a guest. But I think I know what the problem is."

"You do?"

"You miss your father," Ma said. "But it's not my

fault or Jim's that your dad decided to stay in Colorado."

I looked into her eyes. A lump rose in my throat. "Sorry," I said. "I'm going to bed."

I slunk out the back way and over to our house. While my brothers hogged down banana splits, I sat up in bed reading Dad's copy of *Frankenstein*. A car screeched down the street. I looked out the window. Jim Signet was driving himself home.

4

THE MORNING Joey Reid hit me with a rock, Satch and I were standing outside the pickle store.

"Ow!" I screamed, feeling a sharp sting on my ankle. Across the street I saw a boy with hair in his eyes. And a thin piece of sharp brick lay next to my foot.

"What happened?" asked Satch.

I pointed across the street. The boy took aim again.

"Duck!" I shouted.

A rock sailed through the air. Satch ran into the street. A car horn honked. I yanked him back. "Watch out!" A car went whizzing down the avenue.

Satch stood on the curb, panting. The boy was staring across at us. The second rock had missed.

"What's the big idea?" I shouted.

44

The boy cupped his hands over his mouth and yelled—"Zebras!"

I grabbed Satch's hand and started running. "If we're zebras, you're an elephant!" Satch called over his shoulder.

"Why are we running away?" he asked.

"Because I don't want to get hit a second time," I replied, pulling him along. "What do you think Ma would say if we got into a fight?"

We ran all the way up Morris Road. We didn't stop until we got to Bangor Street. There was another long hill before we would reach Lucy Newton.

Satch and I caught our breath. The boy was no-where in sight.

"Haven't we seen that kid before?" I asked my brother.

He nodded. "His name is Joey Reid. He goes to our school."

"I thought I'd seen him somewhere," I said. "He's an Avenger."

Satch's eyes got wide. "I hope the club's not after us for some reason."

"Why should they be?" I said. "I haven't done anything to them. Have you?"

Satch shook his head.

We came up to the school. I looked around for

Joey Reid and didn't see him. We plunged into the crowded front hallway.

"Don't forget you have the dentist after school," I reminded him. I watched him open his locker.

"I do?" said Satch.

"Go straight home," I told him. "Ma will be waiting."

"Where will you be?" asked Satch.

"Explorers Club."

He made a face.

"Better than the Avengers," I said, giving him a pat on the back.

I went up to the second-floor girls' room. There was dried blood on my ankle. I washed it off and went to my own locker. Arthur Cheever was there, blocking my way.

"Give me the password," he said with this stupid grin on his face.

I pushed past. Arthur kept grinning. He was wearing a ski cap, which made his head look even pointier. Before I'd found out he was an Avenger, I hadn't minded how pointy his head was.

"You're too serious," Arthur said, leaning next to me.

"And you and your friends are morons," I said.

He frowned. "Excuse me for trying to be friendly."

"That's a laugh," I said. "I don't know what you've got against my brother Satch and me."

I struggled to open my locker. It was jammed.

"Satch is a cool kid," said Arthur.

I gave my locker a kick. "The next time you want to draw him a picture, do it on a piece of paper," I warned. "Or better still, leave him alone." I pulled up on the handle and the door flew open.

"Satch asked me for an art lesson," said Arthur. "I was just trying to be nice."

"Right," I said, stuffing my jeans jacket inside. I banged the door shut. "Is that what you call siccing Joey Reid on us?"

I walked away and Arthur followed me. "What about Reid?"

"He hit me with a rock."

Arthur snorted. "Reid's really mental. I don't know why Dangerfield has him in the club."

I turned to face him. "Why are you in the club?"

"Because it's cool," Arthur said, shuffling his feet.

"Well, Joey Reid is uncool," I said. "And you can give him that message for me!"

I made it to class in the nick of time. But Arthur walked in two minutes behind me.

Mrs. Jackson turned around from the blackboard. She was wearing a red checkered suit I really liked.

47

"So, you've decided to grace us with your presence, Mr. Cheever?" she said.

"Yeah," said Arthur. He grabbed his ski cap off his head and stuck it in his pocket.

"This is the third time this week you're late," Mrs. Jackson said. "What happened?"

"I was talking to Daughter McGuire in the hall," Arthur blurted out. He grinned at the class.

A soft "oooh" sound snaked through the room. I banged my pencil on the desk. I had enough problems without people thinking that Arthur Cheever and I liked each other.

Mrs. Jackson put up her hands and gestured for quiet. "Let's get focused, people," she said. "Today we're starting a new unit."

I tried to keep my mind on what she was saying. I think that Mrs. Jackson is very smart. The new unit was on family culture. She wanted us to investigate our families. We were supposed to write down family traditions and bring in recipes.

"Should we bring in a family tree?" Connie asked, raising her hand.

"You could try making one with your parents," Mrs. Jackson replied.

"I already have one," said Connie. "I'm a distant relation of Harriet Tubman."

Some of the people in the class clapped.

"How wonderful!" Mrs. Jackson said.

"We don't have a family tree," Anna piped up. "But we have lots of traditions. We eat rice for breakfast and sleep on the floor."

"Can't you afford beds?" quipped Arthur.

The class giggled.

"We sleep on the floor, on futons," Anna explained to him. "Futons are a kind of mattress."

"I should try that sometime," said Mrs. Jackson. Her eyes fell on me. "Think you'll enjoy the new unit, Daughter?"

"I'm not sure," I replied.

"Why not?" she asked.

"I'm not sure my family has any culture," I confessed. "My grandfather was born in Italy and doesn't like pizza."

"Every family has its own culture," said Mrs. Jackson. "And culture isn't only the big, obvious things like the food you eat. It's also the little things. Special traditions that maybe only your family has. Special songs that they sing and places that your family might like to visit. And every family has its own history."

"What kind of history?" I asked.

"The personal history of people," she replied.

"Stories—perhaps about your grandparents or even your great-grandparents. Why don't you start there? I bet you'll come up with some fascinating things to share with us."

"I'll try," I promised.

Mrs. Jackson smiled. She has a great big smile, with lots of teeth. . . .

After school that day Connie, Anna, and I went back to Topknot Cave. The first thing we did was clear out our back entrance. We dragged away a heavy fallen limb at the door and scooped out a glut of wet leaves and old trash. Then we raked the ground at the front and the back with an old tree branch.

"Now we're ready for our second meeting of the Explorers Club," said Connie, brushing her hands off.

"Where's the flashlight?" I asked.

"We don't need it," said Anna. She gave me a poke. "Who's going in first?"

"I did it the last time," I said.

"I have a quarter," said Connie, reaching into her waist pouch. "Why don't we flip for it?"

I wound up the loser.

I got down on my hands and knees and crawled

in carefully. Anna and Connie were on their hands and knees, following me. The floor felt drier that day.

"Smells like snow in here," I said, taking a sniff. My voice sounded muffled.

"It hasn't snowed all year," I heard Connie say.

"Smells like berries and pinecones," said Anna.

I crawled into the middle and felt the cave's smooth insides. A huge shaft of light fell in through the back.

"It's a lot less spooky than it was the other day," I announced.

Anna and Connie scooted up to me. We huddled into a circle with our knees touching.

"We have to keep this place a secret," whispered Connie.

"Whoever tells gets zonked," said Anna.

"What's 'getting zonked' mean?" I asked.

She made a gesture of cutting a throat. "Out of the club, for life," Anna replied. Though the cave was filled with shadows, I could see a gleam in her eye.

"How come you have to act so tough all the time?" I asked.

She shrugged. "Because I am tough."

"I wish I was tough," I said. "I may have to take on the Avengers."

"The Avengers?" said Connie. "How come?"

"I think they might be after Satch and me."

51

"What makes you think so?" asked Anna.

"This morning one of their club members, Joey Reid, hit me with a rock," I explained.

"That's rotten," said Connie.

"He's such a little nerd," said Anna.

"He called me a zebra," I said. "Isn't that stupid?"

Anna wrinkled her nose and Connie looked at the ground.

"I wonder why he did that," I said.

"Yes, I wonder why too," Connie said quietly.

Anna cocked her head and stared at me. "Do you know what it means?"

"Everybody knows what a zebra is," I replied.

They gave each other a look, then looked away.

"Is there some other meaning for the word *zebra*?" I asked.

"A zebra is what they call kids who are half black and half white," said Anna. "Don't tell me you haven't heard that before?"

My heart knocked in my chest. "I never heard it in my old school," I said. "I think it's really stupid. Who does that little name-caller think he is?" I said.

"Somebody told me his mother had quintuplets and murdered them," said Anna. "I also heard that his father's in jail."

"I'm surprised that he, of all people, would call you a zebra," said Connie.

"Could you shut up about it, please?" I said.

"Sorry," said Connie.

We were quiet for a few minutes. Connie reached into her pocket. "Why don't we have some Life Savers Holes?" Anna and I put out our hands and she gave us some candy.

"I told you, you should call yourself something," Anna said, picking up the subject again. She sucked her candy loudly. "If you would say you're African-American or Italian or something, nobody could call you a zebra."

"Some people are prejudiced against African-Americans and Italians too," Connie chimed in. "People can be prejudiced against you no matter what you are. You just have to be different from them."

"I know," said Anna. "But being a zebra is extremely differ—"

"I get the picture," I said, cutting her off.

"Shh!" Connie jerked at my arm. "There's somebody outside," she whispered. We crawled closer to the front entrance and peeked. A big man was standing at the edge of the woods. He was wearing a jacket that was too small for him and eating a sandwich.

"He must be seven feet tall," Connie whispered, ducking back in.

"What's he doing here?" I said, still straining to see.

"What does it look like?" Anna snickered. "He's eating his dinner. He's so fat, he's probably on his sixth sandwich."

"Maybe he was at church," I said.

"He's probably in one of those rehab programs they have for all the people on drugs," Anna said knowingly.

"Maybe he's just taking a walk," said Connie.

"This guy is a giant," I said. I watched him eat his sandwich. Then he snarfed down a candy bar and threw the wrapper on the ground.

"Somebody should tell him not to be a litterbug," said Connie. She touched my arm lightly. "What should we do? Wait for him to leave, or come out now?"

"Let's go," said Anna, getting up on her knees. "We'll just ignore him."

Connie and I came out behind her. My legs had fallen asleep again. The man stood in one spot and watched us. When I was putting on my knapsack, I caught his eye. He didn't look away from me.

I thought about saying hi, but I didn't.

The giant didn't speak either.

"This neighborhood is full of weirdos," I said as he walked away through the trees.

જ-જ-જ

When I got home, nobody was there. Ma had left a note: *At the dentist. Have snack.*

I went next door and found Grandpa Luck in the basement.

"Can I go see Grandma McGuire?" I asked.

Grandpa was fixing a radio and Rasputin was out on his perch. "Love ya, honey!" the parrot screeched.

"I know how to get there," I shouted over the squawking. "Ma lets me go by myself, on the Metro."

"Where's Satch?" said Grandpa.

"At the dentist."

"I thought he was with you," my grandfather said.

"He's at the dentist, Grandpa. Ma left me a note."

Grandpa let me go.

ൟൟൟ 5 ൟൟൟ

"You're just in time to help me change the light bulbs," said Grandma McGuire.

"It is kind of gloomy in here," I remarked, coming into the apartment.

"Just what I was thinking," Grandma McGuire said, "but now you're here to brighten things up." She took my jacket and hung it in the hall closet. The last time I'd seen my grandmother, she'd been taller. Now it seemed as if we were just the same height.

"I think I've grown," I remarked.

"And I've shrunk," she said. "Hear anything from that dad of yours?"

I walked into the dimly lit living room. "Ma thinks he has a reality problem," I said.

"Because he ran away to the mountains to write a book? . . . Your dad was pretty down and out when he lost his teaching job. And writing is something that's always been very important to him." She took a

56

stepladder out of the closet and pulled it into the room. "He'll be in touch soon. Don't worry."

She motioned me up the ladder. I unscrewed the globe from the ceiling light and handed it down. Then I took out three burned-out light bulbs.

"Did Dad tell you when he'd be back?" I asked.

"No," she answered, handing me fresh bulbs one by one. "Now, the fixture . . ."

I screwed the globe back on and climbed down.

"Good job," Grandma said. She folded the ladder, then hit the wall switch. The whole room lit up.

"Ah." She sighed. "That's better." She hurried toward the kitchen. "Now you'll eat something."

"How come you were in the dark?" I asked, following her.

"I was afraid I'd fall off the ladder," she confessed. "Old bones break easily. What do you want to eat?— yummy leftover chicken chow mein or matzo brei?"

"Matzo brei."

I sat down at the kitchen table and stuck my elbows onto the plastic table cover. Grandma McGuire broke up the matzos. Then she put the broken matzos in a bowl and dampened them with water. After that she got out a skillet, some eggs, and some butter.

"Maybe I should come and live with you," I said. "Think so?"

57

"You'd have someone to change your light bulbs and I'd eat matzo brei every day."

She gestured with her elbow. "Get another bulb from the pantry. The lamp on the bedroom side-table needs one."

"You could have changed that one yourself," I said, taking a new bulb. "You don't have to climb a ladder to reach a table lamp."

"Just got out to buy the light bulbs today," Grandma explained. "I don't get out as much, now that my eyes are so bad." I went into the back bedroom and changed the bulb. A picture of my family was on the night table. Grandma McGuire had taken it at the Monument Grounds, during cherry-blossom time a few years ago. Ma and Dad looked much younger. Satch was only three and Jerry Lee was a baby. And both my front teeth were out.

Next to that was another photo of Grandpa Mc-Guire. And standing next to that was the plastic Saint Christopher that always used to ride in my grandmother's car.

"How come you keep this?" I asked. I had brought the Saint Christopher statue back to the kitchen with me.

Grandma McGuire rubbed the head of the saint carrying the child. "It belonged to your grandfather," she said.

"But you're not Catholic," I pointed out. "You're Jewish."

She shrugged. "So? I still like it. And all those years it sat on the dashboard of the Plymouth."

I put the statue on the table and my grandmother served me steaming matzo brei with maple syrup.

"Is matzo brei a tradition?" I asked, blowing on my plate.

"For lots of us," said Grandma McGuire. "When the Jewish people were escaping their bondage in Egypt, they were in such a hurry that they couldn't even wait for their bread to rise. So it came out flat. Like matzos."

I tasted the good food. "Am I Jewish?"

She smiled and wiped her hands on her apron. "Would you like to be?"

"I'm already a lot of other things—Italian, African-American, Irish—"

"Might as well add Jewish to the list," she said. "Nice to be so many things."

"Maybe," I said. "But it might be simpler to be just one thing."

I finished eating and Grandma McGuire gave me seconds. Then she poured herself a glass of hot tea.

"Today somebody hit me with a rock," I said. "He called me and Satch zebras."

She frowned. "That rock must have hurt. What's this zebra thing?"

"Somebody mixed up," I explained, "with black and white. . . ."

"First of all, a zebra is not mixed up," said Grandma. "A zebra is its own kind of animal, a beautiful one."

"But I'm not a zebra!" I said.

"Of course not." She touched my hand. "You're a person—a person who knows exactly who she is. Just remember it. 'Remember who you are,' that's what my father used to say to me."

"Did you remember?" I asked.

"Sure I did," she replied, spooning more sugar into her tea. "I knew who I was better than anybody. Didn't I marry your grandfather? My family wanted me to marry in my own religion. But I didn't. Your grandfather and I liked to read the same books. We liked the same music. We didn't have to be the same religion to get along with one another."

I ran my finger around the edge of my plate. "Did other people pick on you because you're Jewish?" I asked.

Grandma raised her eyebrows. "No," she said. "They picked on your grandfather because he was Irish Catholic."

I threw down my napkin. "Why do people always have to pick on other people?"

Grandma McGuire cleared my plate away and started the dishes. "Maybe because some people aren't sure who they are," she said. "So, they look for other people to push around. That way they can fool themselves into thinking that they're strong."

"But they're not really strong?"

"The strong people are those who really know who they are," she said. "They don't have to prove anything."

The telephone rang. Grandma McGuire went down the hall, then came back a few minutes later. "That was your mother," she said. "You have to go home."

"She probably wonders if I've done my homework," I said.

"Have you?"

"Sort of," I answered. "We have to find out about family traditions, and you told me about matzos."

Grandma's eyes brightened behind her bifocals. "Follow me," she said, heading for the bedroom again. "I have something else that may help."

She opened the top drawer of her dresser and pulled out a small box. "This is for you."

"What is it?"

She handed me the box and I jiggled it.

"Open it," she said.

Between two thin pieces of tissue paper was a shiny gold coin. "Wow," I said. "Is this real gold?"

Grandma McGuire nodded. "Not for spending. But for keeping. My father brought it with him when he came to the United States."

"My great-grandfather? Where did he come from?"

"First he came from Russia," she explained. "He moved to Canada. Then, he came to live in New York. He owned his own bakery. He had lots of friends and they called him Pasha."

She closed the coin into the palm of my hand. "I gave this to your father, but he thought he would lose it. He told me to keep it for you."

"I won't lose it," I promised.

"There's not much else I know about my family's history," Grandma McGuire said. She picked up the black-and-white photo of Grandpa McGuire. "The rest is the life I lived with your grandfather and father."

A car honked outside.

"That must be Ma," I said.

"Oh, your mother was sending a friend to get you," Grandma explained. She peeked through the venetian blinds. "Someone named Jim."

"Is he driving an old limo?" I asked, rushing to the window. Sure enough, Jim Signet's "hearse" was parked at the curb. "How could Ma do this to me? I hate that guy. I think he must hate me too."

"Sorry," she said. She shook her head and tapped her bifocals. "I don't drive anymore."

"That's okay," I said. "I guess I can put up with Jim for a little while."

Grandma McGuire followed me to the hall closet. I gave her a hug. "Thanks for the coin," I said.

She helped me put on my jacket. "Thanks for the sunshine."

6

"How come Ma asked you to come and get me?" I asked. I hadn't seen Jim Signet since the day of the hot sauce.

"She had to drive up to the school. She's trying to get a bead on where your brother is."

"Excuse me?" Why couldn't Jim speak English? I thought.

"Satch didn't show after school. He didn't tell you where he was going, did he?"

"He was going to the dentist with Ma. He was with her—right?"

"If he was, I don't think your mother would be out looking for him," Jim muttered.

My stomach churned as Jim's old Cadillac careened around the corner. Jim gave me a quick glance. "I told your mother I'd cruise a little," he said. "I used to hang out myself, when I was a kid. Maybe I can find him."

"My brother isn't the type to hang out," I said. "If he didn't come home, it means he got lost. Or . . . that something happened to him." I strained to see Jim's face. It was getting dark in the car.

"Don't worry, squirrel," he said. "Satch is probably just playing some basketball."

I started to say that Satch wasn't any good at basketball, when Jim took a turn down Alabama. He seemed to be heading in the direction of Ma's Community Center. "Satch couldn't be this far away from home," I said.

Jim sped past a big playground, then hung a left.

"Sorry," he said. "Just a little detour."

He pulled into a broken-down-looking shopping mall, slammed on his brakes, and got out. The first thing he did was light up a cigarette. Then he walked quickly past a drugstore and a take-out chicken place. He stopped at a boarded-up candy store and knocked on the window. A very large man came out. By now it was dark, so I couldn't see all that well. But there was something about Jim's friend that looked familiar. The two of them talked for a minute. Then the large man handed him something and went back into the candy store. Jim walked back to the car.

"Is this what you call helping my mother look for Satch?" I said as he got in. By now I was really worried.

65

"I told your mother I had to make another stop," he explained. I peered at the envelope he was carrying. There were dollar bills sticking out of it. He put it on the dashboard and started the car.

"Who was that guy you were talking to?" I asked.

"His name's Peanut," said Jim. "He was my main man when we were coming up. His uncle used to run that old candy store. Now Peanut and me are in business together."

"The candy business?" I asked.

Jim gave me a sly look. "Not exactly," he said.

When Jim pulled up in front of our house, I saw a bunch of people on the porch. From the distance I could see that Ma had come back. Maybe she had found Satch, I thought with my heart racing. I jumped out of the car and ran up to the porch. I breathed a sigh of relief. My brother was home, standing next to my mother. But with them were two police officers, a man and a woman.

"Ma!" I caught my mother's arm from behind.

She turned and smiled. "Hi, sweetie." She looked at Satch. "All's well that ends well."

"I got lost," Satch said, looking up at me.

"Lucky for us these officers happened to be cruising," Ma explained. "And Satch flagged them down."

"It was good thinking," said the man officer.

"Your boy got himself lost in a pretty rough neighborhood."

"Exactly where did you find him?" Ma asked.

"Over near the tracks," the woman officer replied. Satch shivered.

"What were you doing over there?" I asked.

"That's where Arthur Cheever lives," he said, looking down at his shoes.

Ma put an arm around of each of us as Jim joined us on the porch. "Go inside with Jerry Lee," she said to Satch and me. "Your grandparents have dinner on in the kitchen."

I stepped into the warm house as Satch bolted past me. "Just a minute," I said, catching his coat collar.

"Let go," he whined.

"Didn't I tell you not to hang out with Arthur Cheever?" I scolded, keeping hold of him. "What were you doing over his way?"

"Hanging out," said Satch, pulling away from me. He stuck his chin out. "How did I know I would get lost? He told me all I had to do was follow the tracks. The problem is, I followed them in the wrong direction."

"You could have gotten run over by a train," I said. "And what were you doing with Arthur?"

"I ran into him on Martin Luther King Avenue," said Satch. "He was going to play some ball and I asked him if I could go. We went to a playground over near his house."

"Is that all you did?" I asked.

"We drew some stuff on the sidewalk with chalk," Satch admitted. "Arthur asked me what kind of ice cream you like."

"What business of that is his?" I fumed. "Keep hanging out with people like Arthur and you're going to be in real trouble," I warned.

Satch threw down his coat. "This isn't my fault. You told me I was supposed to go to the dentist. But when I got home, Ma wasn't here. It was Jerry Lee's appointment today—not mine. So I went down to the pickle store and then—"

"And then you took off with Arthur Cheever. Once you came home, you should have stayed here!"

"Well, you should have stayed here too!" Satch argued.

The door slammed and Ma appeared. Satch and I shut up. The police officers were gone and so was Jim Signet.

"Well, today we really got our signals crossed," Ma said.

"It won't happen again," Satch promised.

"I hope not," she said, giving me a look. "I need to depend on you, Daughter."

"You can," I said, taking my jacket off. "I didn't do anything wrong. I just got mixed up about the dentist."

"I need you to look out for your brother," she said firmly. "I can't be everywhere. Satch is just eight. You're eleven."

"I walk to school with him every morning," I said, plopping down on the couch.

"I want you to walk home with him too."

"For Pete's sake—" I sputtered.

"Daughter keeps a good eye on me as much as she can," Satch piped up.

"I certainly do," I said. "It's not my fault he wanders off with his friends and gets lost."

"Nevertheless, he did get lost," Ma said. "You're his big sister."

"That doesn't mean that I'm his mother," I couldn't help saying.

"From now on," Ma said, "I want you two to walk home together."

I groaned. "Every day?"

She nodded.

"You told me I only had to do that when we first moved here," I argued. "Suppose I want to go somewhere with some of my friends?"

"You'll have to take him with you," said Ma.

"Nothing doing," Satch sputtered, heading toward the stairs. "I don't want to hang out with those Explorers."

"Explorers?" said Ma. "Who are they?"

"It's supposed to be a secret," I said. "Of course it won't be, now that I have to bring my little brother along," I added under my breath.

Ma smiled a tired smile. "Sorry, sweetheart. But I have to count on you. You're the oldest." She turned toward the kitchen. "Wash up for dinner, you two."

Satch and I shared the soap in the bathroom. I eyed him in the mirror. "I'm glad you found your way home," I said.

"Thanks. I'm sorry you have to baby-sit me."

We walked into the kitchen and sat at the table. Jerry Lee was eating carrot sticks, while Grandma and Grandpa Luck made grilled cheese sandwiches. Ma was making hot chocolate. Everybody looked happy. I was happy too. I don't know what I would have done if Satch had been lost permanently or if something bad had happened to him. Still . . . I didn't like it much that from now on, my eight-year-old brother was my responsibility.

𝕀𝕀𝕀 7 𝕀𝕀𝕀

OUT OF the blue Dad came home. One evening there was a knock at the door and he was just standing there with a knapsack full of books on his back and a bag of groceries in his arms. His face was tan and his mouth had a serious look, as if he didn't know what to expect. He had on glasses, which was really strange, because he'd never worn glasses. They were wire rims and they seemed to be a little crooked on his face. Satch, Jerry Lee, and I stood there with our mouths open. Ma had thought it was the newspaper boy coming to collect for the *Post*. She was in the downstairs bedroom, changing out of her work clothes, while I tried to show her my homework. When we heard somebody knocking on the door, she shoved a five-dollar bill into my hand and told me to go answer it.

"You're not the paper boy," Jerry Lee said, looking up at our father.

Dad cracked a smile. "Don't you know me?"

I threw my arms around him, hugging the groceries. I hugged him harder and harder, pressing my head into the paper bag. Jerry Lee jumped up and down. "Mommy! Mommy!" he cried. "It's not 'collect for the *Post*,' it's Daddy!"

By now Dad seemed to be crying. Even though I was still practically glued to him, he managed to reach out for Satch. My brother was standing in the same spot and hadn't moved a muscle.

"I'm so glad to see you guys," Dad said with his voice cracking.

I hugged his arm. "We're glad to see you."

"Take off those glasses," Satch said, turning away. "You look dorky."

Dad stepped inside the house and put down the groceries. Jerry Lee dragged Ma out of her bedroom. She was wearing her old jeans and her hair was falling in her eye.

My parents stared at each other.

"Well, look what the cat dragged in," Ma finally said.

"I started to call, but I thought I'd surprise you," Dad said.

I grabbed his hand. "Won't you stay for dinner?"

He rubbed his chin and looked at Ma. "If it's okay with the chief."

Ma's shoulders relaxed. She walked toward him. They smiled at each other.

"You're welcome to stay," she said. "The kids have missed you."

"Thanks, Tess."

She glanced at the groceries. "What's all that?"

Dad shuffled his feet. "I picked up some stuff at the corner. I didn't want to come empty handed."

"Wow!" I said, diving into the bag. "Ice pops and frozen pizza!"

"Better put that stuff in the freezer before it melts," Ma said.

Satch grabbed the pizza box out of my hand and headed for the kitchen. He rolled his eyes as he passed Dad. "You look weird in those things," he said, pointing to the wire rims.

Dad took his glasses off. "I did a little damage to my sight in Colorado."

Ma lifted an eyebrow. "Strained yourself writing the great novel?"

I drew in my breath. My mother was really angry about my dad's book. He had stayed in Colorado writing instead of coming back right away.

"I've had time to think," Dad said, skipping over Ma's question. He sat down on the couch and pulled Jerry Lee onto his lap. "I haven't just missed the kids, Tess. . . ."

Later that night Dad came up to my room and tucked me in. He sat on the side of my bed and we talked, just the way we used to.

"What is your book about?" I asked.

"About a bunch of people in my head," said Dad. "I'm not writing it now. There are more important things to think about."

"Like what?" I asked.

He touched my hair. "Like you and your brothers," he said, "your mother and Grandma McGuire. All the people I love."

"We've missed you," I said again. "I thought the car might have broken down on the highway. The Rabbit is pretty old."

"I'm afraid the red Rabbit died on me outside of Chicago," Dad said.

"Oh, no!"

"Sorry," said Dad. "I know you liked that car."

"That's okay," I said, "as long as you came back." I took the coin out of the box in my nightstand. "Look what Grandma McGuire gave me."

Dad rubbed the gold piece. "That's your good luck from my side of the family. Don't lose it."

I caught his hand. "Are you coming to live with us?"

He shook his head. "This place your mother has rented is a bit small."

I sat up on my elbow. "Can't we move back to our old house?"

"The new tenants are living there. But I've got a plan," he whispered.

"What plan?" I whispered back.

Dad's eyes twinkled behind his wire rims. His eyes are green. His hair is reddish brown and his ears stick out.

"I haven't worked out all the kinks," he said. "But if I have my way, our family will be together again."

8

RIGHT AFTER that we had another run-in with Joey Reid. Satch and I were in the doughnut store. Connie was with us that morning. She'd spent the night on Cedar Street with her grandmother, because her mother was working the night shift.

"Aren't you going straight to school?" she asked when Satch and I turned down Morris Road the wrong way.

"I never do," Satch bragged. "You have to be slick about it, so nobody will notice, though."

"Oh, Ma notices," I said. "Only she thinks you're safe now that I'm your official bodyguard."

We stopped at the bakery on Mountain View Place. The doughnuts are good there. You can smell their aroma a whole block away. Joey Reid was standing smack dab at the counter. His face was smeared with icing and he was fishing around in his pocket. "Hey, cow pie," he said to Satch.

"Hey, rat," Satch dared to answer. "What's the matter? Can't you pay for your doughnut?"

Making an ugly face, Joey plunked two coins on the counter. I hadn't realized how much shorter he is than I am. I couldn't believe that he'd made me so afraid. Of course, he didn't have a rock in his hand this time.

"What are you staring at?" Joey sneered at me.

"At your silly-looking face," I ventured. I glanced at Connie and Satch. Connie seemed nervous, but Satch gave me a look as if he was proud of me.

"Your mother wears combat boots," Joey said, stuffing his doughnut into his mouth. His long hair fell over his eyes like a curtain. I was boiling inside.

"Don't throw any more rocks at me and my brother," I warned, facing him.

"Let's not get into a fight," whispered Connie.

"Who's interested in fighting?" I said loudly. I thought we were pretty safe, as long as we were in the store. I peered at Joey's head. "I bet you have lice in there."

"And you've got cockroaches in your ears." He stuck out his tongue. It was full of chocolate dough-nut.

"Yuck," said Connie. "Let's go."

"Yeah, go," said Reid, pointing to the door.

"You go," I said, breathing hard. "I'm not going until I buy my doughnut."

"Better watch out," Satch piped up. "My father works for the FBI."

"He does?" said Connie.

"He goes after juvenile offenders," Satch said, giving Joey a stare.

Joey lifted an eyebrow. The woman selling the doughnuts cleared her throat loudly.

"Right," said Joey, wheeling away, "and my mother is Mrs. America."

He left and I breathed a sigh of relief. When I picked up my jelly roll, my hands were shaking.

"I wonder if he believed that story about the FBI," Satch said.

"Isn't it true?" Connie asked.

"Not really," I said. "But I do think that Dad would be awfully mad if he knew that Joey was bothering us."

On our way to school we saw a weird painting on the sidewalk. It looked like a purple cockroach. "That's Joey's mark," Satch pointed out. We made sure to stomp all over it.

✿✿✿

Mrs. Jackson started the day with social studies. I had brought in my good-luck coin to show everybody.

"So who is this Pasha dude?" Arthur Cheever asked, after I'd shown them the coin.

"All I know is that he was a baker," I answered.

Arthur smirked. "And how much is the coin worth? That is, if it's real gold." The class began tittering.

"It's gold," I said.

"How do you know?" Anna piped up.

I glared. I had expected a fellow Explorer to believe me. "Because my grandmother said so," I said.

"Well, how does she know?" Arthur prodded. "If that's real gold, it's worth boo-coo money. You could cash it in if you liked."

"It's worth five thousand dollars," I blurted out.

"That's ridiculous," said Anna. "Why would you bring something worth five thousand dollars to school?"

"Because I wanted to show it to you," I said. I put the coin in my pocket and rubbed it.

Mrs. Jackson walked up to my desk. "Thanks for sharing with us, Daughter. Some things are so special that it doesn't matter how many dollars they're worth. Some things, like your coin, are priceless."

I felt guilty, but I still smiled.

That afternoon Satch had to go to the Explorers Club with us.

"How come he has to go along?" Anna asked. She gave me a cranky look. Satch was crossing the street with us.

"She's my bodyguard," he quipped.

Connie linked her arm through Anna's. "Satch got in trouble the other day. So Daughter has to keep an eye on him."

"Let's go," Satch said. "I want to see Topknot."

Anna turned to me. "You told him?"

"I had to," I said. "Otherwise he wouldn't have come. And if he couldn't have come, I couldn't have come either."

"What's the big deal?" Connie said. "Why do we have to keep it a secret?"

"Sure," Anna said, flouncing away from us, "tell the whole world about our club."

We headed up the driveway and into the woods. A lot more leaves had fallen, so the path was covered with them. The autumn weather had been cold for a while, but now it was hot again. We showed Satch the lookout rock, then took him to Topknot.

"Wow!" my brother said, running toward the cave. "This is the best!" He poked his head in. "Maybe there's something buried in it."

"Like what?" Anna said, lifting an eyebrow. "A

chest of solid gold coins, worth five thousand dollars?"

"The gold piece my grandmother gave me is real," I insisted.

"How come you don't believe her?" asked Connie.

"I just think if Daughter's family has a gold piece worth five thousand dollars, they would have cashed it in," Anna said, throwing her sweater onto the ground.

Satch whirled around. "Five thousand dollars! Why can't I have some of it? Why did Grandma McGuire give the gold coin to you?"

"I guess because I'm the oldest," I muttered. I opened my Thermos and took a swig of orange juice. "Anyway, the coin is for keeping, not for cashing in."

"Let's have our meeting now," said Connie.

"I want to go inside the cave," said Satch.

"Go on," said Anna. "I dare you to crawl in one end and come out the other."

Satch got down on his hands and knees and crawled through to the other side.

"Your brother has more nerve than you do," said Anna.

"I can do it too," I said, feeling my face get hot.

"Prove it," she said.

I got down on my hands and knees. I stuck my

hand into my pocket and rubbed my coin for good luck. Then I started crawling. I crawled slowly at first, and then quickly. In the middle of the cave it was darker and wider. What if something *was* buried in there? I thought, lunging toward the back entrance. I scraped my knee on a rock and fell on my stomach. The breath was knocked out of me. I grabbed my knee and kept crawling. Being in the cave with Connie and Anna hadn't been so bad. But being in there by myself was another matter. I scrambled toward the back and stuck my head out.

"Was it scary?" Connie asked.

"I felt like I was suffocating," I said. I stood up and took a big gulp of air.

"Gangway," said Anna, barreling out the back door. "Try it," she said to Connie.

Connie walked around front and crawled in slowly. Satch crawled in behind her.

"It is kind of scary," Connie admitted when she crawled out again.

"Not to me," Satch boasted.

Connie jabbed me in the side. "Look," she whispered. "He's here again." She pointed.

The giant was standing at the edge of the woods, eating a candy bar. He seemed not to notice us. We crouched behind the rocks and watched. He finished his candy, dropped the wrapper, and walked away.

"I wonder where he's going," Connie said, coming out in the open.

"Maybe he lives here," Anna said in a spooky voice. "Maybe he lives right here in this cave and we don't know it."

"He can't live here," I said.

"How do you know?" said Anna.

"Because there aren't any candy wrappers," I said, getting up and brushing my hands off.

Connie laughed and Satch grinned.

We left Topknot Cave and headed toward Pitts Place. When we came to the edge of the woods, we saw the giant again. He was standing on the street corner. We stooped behind some bushes to spy on him some more.

"Now what's he doing?" Connie whispered.

"He's just standing there," said Satch.

"Maybe he's a criminal," said Anna. "Maybe he's a drug dealer."

"Maybe he's just waiting for the bus," Connie suggested.

"But he's not standing at a bus stop," I pointed out.

A long car slid down the street and stopped at the corner.

"Hey," said Satch. "There's Jim."

Sure enough, it was Jim's "hearse." The car

stopped and the door on the passenger side opened. The giant got in.

"I told you he was a drug dealer," said Anna. "Only drug dealers ride in those kind of cars."

"Or movie stars," Connie pointed out.

"Jim Signet is definitely not a movie star," I said.

The car slid down the street with the two men inside. We came out from behind the bushes.

"I think that guy's name is Peanut," I said, staring into the street.

"No, that's Jim Signet," said Satch.

"No, I mean the other guy," I said. "Once when Jim was driving me home, I think I saw the really big guy give Jim an envelope."

"What kind of envelope?" asked Connie.

I gulped. "An envelope with money in it. Jim and Peanut are in business together."

Anna gasped. "I told you they were drug dealers. Only drug dealers walk around with envelopes of money like that."

"Hey, watch it," said Satch. "Jim Signet's a friend of my mother's."

"That's right," I said. "My mother wouldn't hang out with a drug dealer."

Connie's eyes got wide. "Maybe your mother doesn't know that he's a drug dealer," she whispered.

"My mother's not dumb," said Satch.

"But she is awfully nice," I pointed out. "She's always trying to help people."

"Maybe she's trying to help the drug dealers," said Anna.

"But my mother is a social worker," I said, arguing the other side. "Social workers don't help drug dealers."

"Anyway," Satch added, sticking his chin out, "what do you know about drug dealers?"

Anna tossed her head. "I know just about as much as anybody. It's always on the news."

"Well, Jim is not a drug dealer," Satch insisted.

Anna stepped up to him. "I bet that he is."

"He isn't," Satch argued.

"He is," said Anna.

"Be quiet!" I interrupted. I pulled Satch by the elbow. "Let's go."

"Gladly," said Satch, giving Anna a final glare.

I turned away without saying good-bye.

"See you tomorrow," Connie sang out.

"Later," I said, turning and waving. They kept on down the street, while Satch and I took the alley.

"Do you believe that stuff?" Satch asked.

"I don't know what to believe," I answered. "Jim did say that he and Peanut were partners. And he hasn't even told Ma yet what kind of business he's in."

We walked the rest of the way in silence. It was hard to get the picture of Peanut out of my mind. I also kept remembering the fat envelope. If Jim Signet was a drug dealer, he was probably dangerous. That might mean Ma was in danger. On the other hand, since Dad had come back, we hadn't seen Jim at all. Maybe there was nothing to worry about. Maybe, if we were lucky, we'd never see Jim Signet again.

∾∾∾ 9 ∾∾∾

"PUSH!" said Grandpa Luck. "Now knead it with the palms of your hands." He sprinkled more flour on the board.

"Making bread is hard work," I said, squeezing the dough.

Grandma Luck handed Dad a cup of tea. "Nice that you could visit us for a while," she said.

Dad balanced the cup on his knee. "I'm hoping it will be more than a visit," he said.

Sunlight filled my grandparents' kitchen. Dad had been in Washington for over a week. He still hadn't told us about his plan. But he had been seeing a lot of Satch, Jerry Lee, and me.

Jerry Lee ducked under my arm and stuck his fingers into the bread dough. "Give me a turn," he said, pushing as hard as he could.

Grandma Luck clucked her tongue. "That stuff is going to have more people's hands in it."

Dad chuckled. "The more hands in the dough, the better the bread."

"Move over, snort faces," said Grandpa. "Now it's my turn."

He worked the dough into a fine round ball and rubbed it with butter. He put it in a pan and popped it into the oven.

I sniffed my hands and smelled a nice yeasty smell. "I bet your father and mother taught you how to bake bread that way," I said.

Grandpa shook his head. "I taught myself, from a book."

"Darn," I said. "I was hoping it was a family tradition."

"It is," Grandma Luck said, wiping Jerry Lee's fingers. "Only, it's not a tradition that was handed down to us. It's a family tradition your grandpa and I started."

"Just like franks and beans on Saturday," Grandpa said, tugging my braid.

"I think Daughter is hoping for something a little flashier than franks and beans," Dad said, sipping his tea. "One of her classmates is a descendent of Harriet Tubman."

"Extraordinary," said Grandpa. "But do you have to be related to somebody famous in order to get a good grade in that school?"

"Actually, the assignment is to collect family stories of any kind," I admitted. "I was just hoping—"

"Just a minute," Grandma Luck interrupted. "There was somebody famous in my family. My uncle Frank was one of the first African-American firemen in Charleston, West Virginia. That's the town where I grew up."

"Was he a famous fireman?" asked Jerry Lee.

"Famous in my family," Grandma Luck said. "Famous in our town too. In those days it was real hard for an African-American to get a job as a fire fighter. It was a big thing just to be considered for a job like that."

"Even if they were really, really good at it? Even if they really wanted to?" asked Jerry Lee.

Grandma Luck shook her head. "Unfortunately. Nowadays, there are more opportunities."

"When I write my family stories, I'll put down Uncle Frank's name," I volunteered.

Dad rubbed my back. "Even though he's not famous?"

"He is famous," I said. "Famous in our family."

Grandma Luck smiled at me. "Well, I've got another story for you."

"You've had your turn," said Grandpa.

"But this is the best story she's going to get," Grandma Luck argued.

Grandpa Luck put his hand up. "You've told about your family. Now I'm telling about mine."

Dad gave me a secret smile. "I think you're going to have more than enough grist for your mill," he whispered.

"Come on, Vincent," said Grandma Luck. "I just want to tell her about—"

"Wait your turn," Grandpa interrupted. "I'm telling her the one about the carnival."

Jerry Lee bounced in his chair. "You were in the carnival?"

"I haven't heard this story in years," Dad remarked.

Grandpa got up in a hurry. "I'll be right back. I need my accordion."

Grandma wiped her face with her apron. "I hope he isn't too long winded."

"I heard that!" Grandpa yelled up from the basement. He came back lugging his instrument.

"Does this story have music in it?" Jerry Lee asked.

"Lots of music," said Grandpa. "When I was a boy, music was a big part of my life."

"A love of music runs in the family," said Grandma, pulling a chair up. "That's probably why Satch is so musical."

Grandpa Luck arranged his accordion on his lap, while Dad took Jerry Lee onto his knee. I grabbed an apple out of the fruit bowl. Then Grandpa Luck played a long, slow riff and began to speak. . . .

"Long ago in the Dark Ages, when I was born, about five hundred years ago—"

"You aren't five hundred years old," interrupted Jerry Lee.

Grandpa Luck chuckled. "Can't fool you, can I?"

"Don't drag it out, Vincent," said Grandma.

Grandpa fingered the keys of his accordion and kept on talking.

"This story has a sad beginning. It begins with the death of my father, who grew up in Italy. When he died, my mother Lucy was very unhappy. She wanted a brand-new life. So she decided to come to the United States on a big boat. Her mother went along with her. And so did I. Only I don't remember the trip, because I was just three. But I do remember my father. I remember the sound of his laugh and his playing for me. His favorite song was the one I'm playing now, 'Santa Lucia.' This accordion belonged to him. . . .

"My mother wasn't very happy her first months in the States. She and my father had loved each other very much. His name was Vincent, like mine. But

Mother was a hard worker and so was my grand-mother. They were determined to make a good life. They moved near some other relatives in New Jersey. One thing led to another and they started a cannery."

"What's a cannery?" Jerry Lee asked.

"A place where they can things," Grandpa explained. "Like vegetables. In this case, Mother and Grandmother had a tomato cannery."

"But you hate tomatoes," I interrupted. "That's why you don't like pizza."

"My mother hated them too," Grandpa continued, "just like some people hate broccoli. Every morning, Mother would get up and cry about it.

" 'What's wrong, Mother?' I'd ask. I was about five by this time.

" 'My life is miserable,' Mother would say. 'Every-where I look there are tomatoes. Outside in the gar-den. In pots on the front porch. On tables in the yard.'

"It was true. My grandmother had taken every square inch of land and planted just that one fruit. She and my mother spent every waking hour tending to them. And when they weren't outside in the gar-den, they were indoors, doing canning. The tomatoes came in bumper crops. They filled up every inch of the kitchen and living room, even the closet. Mother was up at dawn, peeling and slicing and cooking. She spent long hours preparing the cans that the tomatoes were canned in. She canned them whole. She canned them in sauce.

" 'I might as well be a tomato myself,' she confided in me. 'Things might not be so bad if I liked the taste of the things. But even the smell of them makes me sick to my stomach. All of my clothes have tomato spots on them. Yet this is the only way your grandmother and I have to make a living. I hate this tomato life!'

"Of course, all this talk upset me. What child likes to see his mother crying? Now that I'm older, I think it wasn't the tomatoes so much that made my mother sad. I think that she missed my father."

"What happened to her?" I asked. I felt very sorry for Grandpa Luck's mother. "Did she have to can tomatoes the rest of her life?"

"Oh, no," said Grandpa with a smile. "Things took a real turn for the better.

"One day a small carnival came to town. And since my grandmother had a roadside stand next to the cannery, some of the people who worked in the carnival dropped by to buy vegetables.

" 'What gorgeous plump tomatoes,' a young man commented, who happened to be the ringmaster.

"My mother was out at the stand, waiting on him. 'What's so gorgeous about them?' she said. 'Pick them and can them all day long and they won't seem very gorgeous to you. I'd give anything to have an exciting life like you have in the carnival.'

"One thing led to another and my grandmother asked the carnival people to stay for dinner. What a meal Grandmother made! Lots of meat and pasta and vegetables and bread."

"And tomatoes?" asked Jerry Lee.

"Those too," said Grandpa. "The carnival people ate until they almost burst. Then one of them took out a fiddle and played folk songs.

"My mother listened for a long while. Then she went into her room and got my father's accordion. She knew how to play it too. But nobody had heard it since the day my father had died.

"When the carnival fiddlers took a break, my mother Lucy began to play. At first she played sad songs and started to cry. Then she played songs that were happier. And by the end of the evening she had people dancing. And I saw that there was a big smile on her face.

" 'You're a wonderful musician,' the ringmaster said. 'I could use someone like you in the carnival.'

"So my mother took the job. She and I left the

cannery with my father's accordion. And that's how I
came to live with the carnival."

"What did you do there?" Jerry Lee asked. "Were
you a clown?"

"No," my grandfather replied. "I rode horses. I
learned to stand very still on their backs, while they
were still moving. I could even do somersaults on the
back of a horse."

"Wow," I said. "Can you still do that?"

Grandpa shook his head. "Trick riding is something I haven't done in years. I doubt that I remember how."

"So what happens next in the story?" asked Jerry
Lee.

"Five years passed and my mother Lucy and I
went back to the cannery," he answered. "My grandmother was getting old and needed some help. But
I'll always remember our days in the carnival. I'll
never forget the brightness of my mother's music and
the way she smiled when she played."

Grandpa Luck smiled a very big smile. And then
he played "Santa Lucia." The music made me feel all
warm inside.

Dad took off his glasses and sniffed.

"Mm, I smell something wonderful. . . ."

Grandma Luck opened the oven. The fragrance of

the bread filled the room. She took out the crusty brown loaf and set it on the table. We all gathered around, sniffing.

"Don't burn your noses," Grandpa Luck said with a laugh.

Grandma took the bread out of the pan and placed it on a board. My mouth was watering. She got out a knife, some plates, and the butter. Grandpa put down his accordion and cut the loaf into slices, then passed them around to us.

"Yum," said Jerry Lee.

"Delicious," said Dad.

I sank my teeth into the bread and it melted in my mouth.

"Ready to tell your story, Millie?" asked Grandpa Luck.

Grandma Luck tapped my head. "This is a special one for Daughter."

"What's it about?" I asked.

"Where you got your name. . . ."

᪥᪦ᪧ *10* ᪥᪦ᪧ

Grandma Luck's Story

"MANY, MANY years ago there lived a girl called Mary. I've never seen a picture of her. But in my imagination she has long legs and long braided hair and very curious dark eyes. She was very much loved by her mother and father. The family lived in Virginia, although Mary's parents had been born in the western part of Africa. Mary's mother and father didn't come up with the idea of migrating to this country. They were forced to come. Landowners in the New World needed laborers. And some unscrupulous people got the notion of capturing other human beings and selling them as workers. It was a cruel and dirty business we call slavery. Mary's mother and father were among these captives. They were brought to Virginia and sold to the same person. They lived and worked on the same plantation. They married there. And that's where their daughter, the girl called Mary, was born.

"There was only one child in Mary's family. After work in the evening the family would sit outside of their small cottage. Mary and her mother sat on the porch stairs, while Mary's mother braided her hair. Mary's father stooped on the ground, drawing marks in the earth. 'These are your secret marks,' he said to Mary, pointing with his stick. 'Do not forget them.' He touched Mary's bare foot. 'My only daughter is gold to me.'

" 'To me, my only daughter is a cool drink of water,' Mary's mother added. Mary's mother knew the true value of a deep drink from the well, for she worked in the hot sun all day.

" 'I wish I were a piece of gold!' Mary said. 'Then I could buy our freedom. I wish I were a cool drink of water! Because water can go where it wants to.'

" 'She's right, you know,' said Mary's mother. 'There are places in this country where it is against the law to enslave people. Others have escaped. Why can't we try it?'

" 'You know my plan,' said Mary's father. 'Be patient.' Mary's father was a blacksmith, who was allowed by his owner to hire himself out to other people. Every time he earned wages, he could keep a portion of them. He was hoping to save enough money to purchase his freedom and the freedom of his family someday.

" 'Suppose we die before enough money is saved?' Mary's mother said. 'Suppose they decide to separate us?'

" 'That won't happen,' said Mary's father. 'We must be patient. We will be free someday.'

" 'But when?' asked Mary. 'I would like to be free by Christmas!'

"Her father smiled sadly. 'I think we'll have to wait a bit longer than Christmastime,' he said.

"But the family could not afford to wait. The owner of the plantation made a sudden decision. He was going to break up Mary's family. Mary was nearly eleven. She was strong and big for her age. The owner of the plantation needed money. So he decided to sell her.

"When Mary's mother heard the news, she wept. She and her husband tried to keep the news a secret.

" 'I will not let them take away my only treasure,' Mary's mother whispered that night. 'We must run away. I would rather die than lose my daughter.'

"Mary's father stared up at the ceiling. 'I think there is someone who might be able to help us,' he whispered back to his wife.

"There was a doctor in the town that Mary's father knew. He was fair-minded and it was rumored that he worked with the Underground Railroad.

99

Mary's father secretly met him in a barn and spoke with him about his family's situation.

" 'I have some money saved,' he told the doctor, when there was no one else around to overhear. 'If there's a way you can help us to escape, I would be grateful.'

"The doctor shook hands with him. 'I'll see what I can do to make the arrangements,' he said.

"On Christmas Eve, while the owners of the plantation were having a big celebration, Mary's family slipped away. They traveled through the woods with a guide who worked with the Underground Railroad. They hid in barns and cellars. They were making their way toward freedom.

"The so-called owners of the family were furious. They had an artist draw pictures of Mary and her mother and father from memory. Then they placed the pictures in stores and post offices in the neighboring towns.

"Once the family was traveling through a town, in a hay wagon. They were wearing hats and capes to conceal their faces and the farmer who was helping them escape had stacked hay in the back of the wagon all around them. Well out of town, they stopped at a creek for a drink of water. Mary got out and dipped her hands into the icy water. She took a long drink. Then she left her parents and the driver for a moment and walked along the side of the creek, watching the ice floes. Suddenly, a rider galloped up out of nowhere. Mary's parents called her, but it was too late. The man had cupped his hand over Mary's face. He forced her to get onto his horse with him. Mary struggled, but the man was stronger. By now her father had jumped in front of the horse. Her mother was crying. 'Take me instead!' she screamed. Mary watched in horror as the rider's horse almost trampled her father. Tears streamed down her face as she was carried away, her parents growing small in the distance. She had been free on Christmas Day. But now her freedom had ended.

"Mary was taken back to the plantation where she was born. As the owners had planned, she was sold. She was taken to Washington, D.C., to work with a new family as the baby-sitter. All day long, every day, she thought of her parents and how much she missed them. She wondered if they had been caught again also. She wondered if she would ever see them again.

One Sunday, when she was outside of a church, minding the children of the people she worked for, a young minister came up to her.

" 'Did you lose this?' he asked, sticking a small blue book beneath her nose.

"Mary was shocked. She was not allowed to own a book. How could the book the young minister was offering possibly belong to her?

" 'Perhaps it belongs to your mistress,' the young man insisted. 'Let's look inside.' He opened the book and showed it to her. Mary peered at it. The strange markings danced in front of her eyes. But inside the front cover, there was a set of marks she recognized. Mary's heart pounded. They were her own secret marks that her father had drawn in the earth for her. The young man touched her hand. 'All is well with your mother and father,' the young man whispered. 'They are no longer in captivity.'

"Mary did not know whether to laugh or cry. For the first time in weeks she felt happy. At least the dream of freedom had come true for her parents.

"There were other Sundays when she was told to wait outside of the church. When the service was over, her owners would send out their children. Mary was to mind them while the grown people socialized. On these Sundays the young minister always came out and passed by her, but never said anything. Mary wondered if he had more news of her parents, though she didn't dare ask him. However, the day came when the young minister spoke with her a second time. 'Fetch us some water,' he said, shoving a pitcher into her hand. Mary was surprised at his sternness. She walked to the well and the young minister followed.

" 'Be ready next Thursday,' he whispered when they were away from the crowd. 'I will call at the house where you work. Slip out and hide in the carriage. My wife will be there.'

"Mary hardly dared breathe. Suppose the minister was only tricking her? How did she know she could really trust him? Then she remembered the secret marks in the blue book. The marks could only have been made by her father. If the minister wanted her to slip away on Thursday, it must also be her parents' wish. Mary decided to take a chance.

"That Thursday the minister's carriage stopped at the house. Mary left the children in the nursery, put on her cape, and slipped out the back way. The minister was in the downstairs parlor, talking to her owners. But the minister's young wife was waiting outside. She beckoned Mary into the carriage and had her hide on the floor. Then the driver took them quickly back to the church. The minister's wife directed Mary to a room in the cellar. A disguise of boys' clothing was waiting: a hat, trousers, and a jacket, even a pair of boys' boots.

" 'Put these on,' the woman said hurriedly. 'I have to go back to pick up my husband.'

"Mary dressed quickly and waited. It seemed like

an eternity until the young minister and his wife got back.

" 'We'll have to cut your hair,' the minister said. Mary clutched her braids.

" 'Don't worry, it will grow back,' the minister's wife said. She picked up the scissors. 'But you must pretend that you are a boy for a while. My husband is going on a trip north.'

" 'You will pretend to be my servant,' the minister explained. 'From now on you must answer to the name Joshua.'

"Mary traveled north with the young deacon. She never spoke to anyone, because the sound of her girlish voice might give away her identity. She wore boys' clothes and pretended to be the minister's young manservant. She and the minister traveled by boat and by train. She often felt people staring at her. She was frightened. What if she was recognized and captured again? What if something happened and she was prevented from seeing her parents once more? On the last leg of her journey the young minister left her. He took her to the home of an older couple in Massachusetts.

" 'Wait here for a few days, Joshua,' the young minister said. His eyes twinkled when he called her Joshua. 'All will be well. These people are friends.'

"But Mary was frightened. There were many visitors to the old couple's home. Mary kept wearing her boys' clothing and spoke to no one. When the old woman of the house called her by her real name, she didn't answer. She continued to answer only to the name Joshua.

"One morning the woman of the house called her. 'Joshua, come into the parlor.' Mary came in and stood stiffly. She pulled her cap down over her eyes. The old woman disappeared. After a few moments Mary heard footsteps in the front hallway, and voices she recognized. Her mother and father appeared in the doorway.

"Mary's heart leapt, but her body was frozen. It had been so long since she'd seen her parents. She had almost begun to give up hope. Maybe it wasn't really happening, she told herself. Maybe it was only a dream that her mother and father were standing right there in front of her.

" 'Madam, sir . . .' The old man of the house was talking to her parents. 'I believe this is your child.' He pointed to Mary.

"Her father stared. 'But this is a boy. It is a daughter I came for.'

" 'I am your daughter! It's me!' Mary blurted out. She had found her tongue again. She tossed off her cap and ran toward her parents. 'See!' she cried, throwing herself into their arms.

"Her mother and father hugged and kissed her. Mary began to cry.

"The old couple chuckled. 'She put on such a good act, I had begun to believe she really was a boy,' the old man said.

"Mary and her parents thanked the couple. They went on their way to the new home Mary's parents had made for them. Three free people.

"To mark the beginning of her new life Mary re-named herself. The secret marks her father had taught her spelled the word *daughter* in Arabic. So Daughter is what Mary decided to call herself. She was the very first Daughter in our family."

Grandma Luck turned and looked at me. She had tears in her eyes.

I felt something settle inside me. It was the power of my name.

∞∞ 11 ∞∞

"Your grandmother Luck is a good storyteller," Dad said. We walked across the yard home. Jerry Lee was chewing a piece of bread. I was still under the spell of my grandparents' stories.

I felt for Dad's hand. "The first Daughter was so brave," I said.

"You're brave too," he said, squeezing my pinkie.

"Not that brave," I said. I thought about my ancestor—the girl my own age, who had the same name as me; the girl whose parents had been born in Africa. She had traveled all by herself along the Underground Railroad. I was such a chicken that I'd run away when Joey Reid threw a rock at me. I was afraid of the dark in Topknot Cave and dreamed about skeletons.

Jerry Lee tugged Dad's elbow. We were climbing the stairs to our back porch. "What about your family stories, Dad?" my youngest brother asked.

Dad took off his glasses. "I can't think of any."

"But you're a writer," I said. "You must have lots of stories."

Dad shook his head. "Those are only made-up stories in my mind. Not about real people."

We sat down on the back stairs. The walk was slick with wet yellow leaves. Ma's car still wasn't back.

"We can go inside," I said, moving closer to my father. "Ma wouldn't mind. She knew you were coming to visit us at Grandma Luck's this morning."

Dad eyed the back door. "Let's stay out in the air," he said. He reached into the corner of the porch for an old tennis ball. He popped it up and caught it, then let out a chuckle. "There is one thing I remember that my dad told me. . . ."

"What is it?" asked Jerry Lee.

Dad tossed him the ball. "It seems I had two great-aunts in Ireland. I never met them, of course—since I was born here. These two ladies were named for the colors they wore."

I laughed. "What were their names? Red and Green?"

"Close," Dad said. "Pink and Blue."

Jerry Lee giggled. "Those are silly names."

"They were twins," Dad explained. "Their parents dressed them that way to tell them apart."

"And the names stuck?" I said.

Dad grinned. "They took their names very seriously. And all their lives they wore only those two colors."

"What did they name their children?" I joked. "Orange and Green?"

Dad got up and stretched. "They never had their own kids. But they were the village midwives. They delivered other people's children. In fact, they delivered your grandpa McGuire. Everybody thought that Grandpa McGuire was supposed to be a girl."

"How come?" asked Jerry Lee.

"Because when he was ready to be born, Pink was the first one to arrive. That was the superstition going around the village. If Pink got there first, the family was supposed to have a daughter."

"Well, that does it," I said with a giggle. "I'm not like the Irish side. My favorite colors are black and purple."

"And mine is yellow," Jerry Lee piped up.

I tugged at Dad's hand. "What was Grandpa McGuire like?"

Dad rubbed my head. "He was a great guy. What can I say? He was my father."

"Did he act Irish?"

"I suppose he spoke like he was from Ireland.

And once in a blue moon he'd play on the pipes. But he wasn't big on old traditions."

"When you were a child, who were you the most like?" I asked him. "Were you Irish like your father or Russian Jewish like Grandma McGuire?"

Dad shrugged. "Like neither one of them, I guess. Or maybe like both. Mom and Dad kind of combined their family traditions."

I lifted an eyebrow. "You mean Grandpa McGuire played the bagpipes while Grandma McGuire was making matzo brei?"

He chuckled. "Something like that. Mainly they were very busy with their work as union organizers."

I looked up at Dad. "Who am I like?" I asked.

"Like yourself—aren't you?"

"That's not what I mean." I touched my face. "I want to know who I am. Am I African-American, like Grandma Luck and Mom? Am I Italian-American, like Grandpa Luck? Am I Irish like you? Am I Russian like Grandma McGuire? Am I white? Am I black? What am I?"

Dad stood back and gave me the once-over. "Hmm," he said with a twinkle in his eye, "you look like a human being to me. A girl human being, about eleven."

I laughed in spite of myself. But then I said, "This isn't a joke, Dad. Do you want me to be a nothing for the rest of my life?"

"You could never be a nothing," he said, giving me a pat on my back.

Jerry Lee waddled up. "Can I look at television?"

"Sure," Dad said, watching him go into the house. "If your mama and Satch don't come back from the dentist soon, Daughter and I will come inside and fix some lunch for us. Okay?"

"Okay," Jerry Lee said, letting the door bang.

Dad turned to me.

"What's all this talk about who you are, all of a sudden? Kids at your new school been giving you trouble?"

"One boy called me a zebra," I told him. "A zebra is someone mixed with black and white."

He winced and squeezed my hand. We walked out into the yard. "See that tree?" he said, pointing up at our maple. "Once it had green leaves. Now, its leaves are yellow. Was it any better when the leaves were green? It's still the same tree."

"I'm not a tree, Dad," I said. "I need to know what to call myself."

"But you're so many things," he said. He waved his hand in the air. "Race is only an idea that some

111

person invented. Some person who needed to put people in little boxes."

"And I'm a hundred trillion of those little race boxes. I don't want to be mixed up," I said. "I want to call myself something."

"Then call yourself everything," said Dad. "Or call yourself one thing. It's up to you to decide."

"You really don't get it," I said.

"Maybe I don't get it," Dad admitted. "But there is something I do know. You are the best of everything I am and the best of your mother.

"You're the best of all our great-grandmothers and great-grandfathers," he said, putting his arms around me. "But the most important part of the recipe is who you are as an individual."

"But what if there's a war between the races?" I insisted. That was a fear that I'd never told to anyone.

"That isn't going to happen here," Dad said.

"But what if it does?" I argued. "Which side would I be on? How would I decide?"

He touched my cheek. "The same way I would decide," he said. "By my conscience. Certainly not by my color."

Dad stroked my hair. I wanted to be the kind of person who did things by her conscience. I wanted to be brave, like the first Daughter.

Ma pulled up in the alley and Satch jumped out of the car. "I got a new tooth!" he cried. He came right up to me and grinned in my face. In the front of his mouth there was a new, shiny white chomper. Satch reached up and pulled at it.

"I can even take it in and out," he bragged.

I clapped my hands. "Great!" I said.

"That's a neat trick," said Dad. He knelt down in front of my other brother. "Put it back in and say 'cheese.'"

"Cheese!" cried Satch, putting the tooth in again.

Ma came up behind us. "How was the visit?" she asked.

Dad stood up. "Okay. Bread baking at your mom and pop's, and then Daughter and I had a good talk." He patted my shoulder. "I think we helped her out on that family-history assignment. Right, honey?"

"Right," I said, snuggling in closer.

Ma and Dad looked at each other.

"I think Dad could help me out some more," I volunteered.

"I was just about to open a can of soup for Jerry Lee," Dad said.

Ma cracked a thin smile. "What kind of soup?"

Dad's face got red. "I thought you might have some split pea in the cabinet."

"That's your favorite kind of soup," I said to Ma.

"But maybe your mother doesn't want me to stay," said Dad.

"Of course you can stay," I answered for my mother. I gave Ma a pleading look. "Can't he, Ma?"

Ma's face relaxed. "Why not?" she said. "After all, we don't know how much longer your father will be in these parts. And I've—I mean, you kids have missed him."

We started toward the back porch. Dad gave me a wink. Then he caught up with my mother. I saw him touch her arm. She didn't pull away. Satch ran shouting into the house, ahead of all of us.

"Hey, Jerry Lee! Come and see my new tooth! This is my lucky day! I ain't a 'snag' anymore!"

It was a lucky day. Some things that were very hard to understand seemed to be slowly coming together.

ҩ҉ 12 ҩ҉

MA ENDED up inviting Dad for Thanksgiving dinner. Everything seemed perfect, until I discovered my gold piece was missing. On Thanksgiving morning I took the box out of my nightstand. But all I found inside were the thin pieces of tissue paper. I looked in the pockets of all of my jeans. Then I looked in my knapsack. I even looked in the washing machine. I looked under my bed and found my beaded belt that had been missing, along with lots of dust balls. But there was no lucky coin.

"Have you seen my gold coin?" I asked, going into my brothers' room.

"The one worth five thousand dollars?" said Satch. He was putting on his red bow tie. Ma had made him and Jerry Lee bathe first thing that morning. Jerry Lee was sitting in short gray flannel pants, looking unhappy.

"These pants are itchy," said Jerry Lee.

"This is serious," I said, ignoring my youngest brother. I grabbed Satch's shoulders. "It's not worth five thousand dollars, but I'm in big trouble if I don't find it. Grandma McGuire's coming today."

"How much is it worth?" Satch said.

I pointed my finger at him. "If you snitched that gold piece . . ." I warned.

"What do you think I am?" said Satch. "A thief? Anyway, I wouldn't know who to sell it to."

Ma caught me at the top of the staircase. She had her terry-cloth robe slung over her shoulder. I guess she was going into the bathroom for a shower.

"Where are you going?" she asked. "Have you showered? Why aren't you dressed?"

"I have to go see somebody," I said, passing by in a hurry.

"Your father's coming over to help with the cooking," Ma called after me. "I need you to set the table. There are some pretty mums I brought home last night from my office. I thought they'd go well as a centerpiece."

"Okay," I yelled, going out the front door. I ducked across the street. I was hoping that Connie was already at her grandmother's house, since it was Thanksgiving Day.

I knocked on the door. Somebody peeked

through the venetian blinds. Then the front door opened and Connie slipped out.

"Happy Thanksgiving," she said. Her bangs had been curled and she was wearing a brown velvet dress with matching bow in her hair. "Are you having an early dinner? We are. Don't tell me that your mother is letting you wear jeans?"

I looked down at my clothes. They were rumpled. I had hardly washed my face that morning.

"Have you seen my good-luck piece?" I asked.

"The one from your Russian ancestor?" said Connie.

"Yes. Maybe I left it in school in my desk. What do you think?"

"It would have been stupid to leave something worth five thousand dollars at school. Somebody would steal it."

"It's not worth five thousand dollars," I confessed.

"Then why did you say it was?" Connie asked.

"Because—because Arthur and Anna didn't act as if they thought the coin was special. I just said it, that's all."

Connie moved around on the stoop, trying to warm up. "When is the last time you saw the coin?"

I thought for a moment. "It might have been at school."

"Remember what Arthur Cheever said about cashing it in somewhere?" she reminded me.

"Do you think Arthur Cheever stole it?" I exclaimed.

She shivered. "How should I know? I have to go in now. My grandmother asked me to open the cranberry sauce. I have to put it in a special dish. It has to chill in the refrigerator." She touched my hand with her cold fingers. "Happy Thanksgiving. Maybe we can get together later."

"I can't," I said. "After we eat, we have to go help Ma pass out dinners."

I went back home and got dressed. I tried not to think about the gold coin. Dad arrived in a taxi with Grandma McGuire. Grandma McGuire was supposed to bring pie, but she'd brought pot roast.

"I had it in the freezer," she told Ma at the door.

She'd also brought a big can of fortune cookies. "For dessert," she said.

"How's the turkey doing?" Dad asked.

"I don't think the drumstick is quite ready to wiggle," Ma answered.

"Let me check it out," Dad said, heading for the kitchen.

Jerry Lee came down in a pair of overalls and a white shirt. Ma had let him change out of his wool shorts. Satch had already taken off his bow tie. I was wearing my one and only dressy dress, which I love. It's a light violet color.

"What's that big yellow thing in the middle of the table?" Grandma McGuire asked. She squinted.

"Those are mums," I said.

"What?"

"Those are the flowers," I said.

"Very pretty," she said, sinking into the couch. She motioned for me to sit next to her. What if she asked me about the gold piece? I thought. What would I say?

"And who do you think will get the wishbone?" she said, giving me a wink.

"Some very lucky person," I said. I bit my lip. What did I have to bring up the subject of luck for?

She patted my knee. "I feel very lucky today— being here with all of you."

"Excuse me," I said, scooting away. "I have to help Ma and Dad in the kitchen."

My parents were bent over the turkey. Dad had his arm on Ma's back. They looked so perfectly normal.

"Is the drumstick wiggling yet?" I asked. When my mother can wiggle the drumstick, it means the turkey is done.

"Almost," Ma said.

"This is going to be some good bird," Dad said, smiling.

I shot out of the room to find Satch. He was at the front door, letting Grandma and Grandpa Luck in.

"Happy Thanksgiving!" said Grandma Luck, hurrying by with two covered dishes.

"Happy Thanksgiving," I said.

"Gangway!" said Grandpa Luck, pushing past with a big baking dish. "Who likes manicotti, the old-fashioned way?"

"I do!" cried Jerry Lee.

"Doesn't manicotti have tomato sauce in it?" I said.

Grandpa Luck winked. "Yes, but I still love it."

While my grandparents put the food on the table, I pulled Satch into a corner. "I think that this might be the day that Ma and Dad get together," I said.

Satch shook his head. "No way."

"They're wiggling the drumstick together," I argued. "I saw them in the kitchen. Dad was practically kissing her."

"They're too darned different," said Satch. "All Dad does is read and write. Ma is too busy for that stuff."

"But they're not divorced yet," I insisted.

"Dad stayed away too long," he said.

"He had lost his job. He was writing a book."

Satch smirked. "And now what's he going to do?"

I pulled him closer. "He has a plan," I whispered.

Satch's eyes shifted. "Does Ma know about it?"

"I'm not sure," I said with a swallow.

He put his hands on his hips. "They're still not getting together again."

I put out my pinkie. "Bet you five dollars."

"Fine," said Satch, hooking my finger. "You'll be sorry when you lose your money."

For dinner that day we had corn pudding, rolls, manicotti, turkey, stuffing, sweet potatoes, collard greens, pickles, pot roast, and fortune cookies. We had apple cider and milk to drink.

The first thing that happened was that we opened the fortune cookies. My fortune said that someday I would go on a long journey.

The second thing that happened was that Dad dropped the turkey. He was carrying it on a big platter. Ma had opened the kitchen door and he walked out. He must have tripped on the edge of the rug, because the next thing we knew he'd lost his balance and the turkey was sliding off the platter and heading for a landing. Luckily, it hit the mums in the middle of the table.

"Oh, my gosh!" Grandpa Luck cried. He jumped out of his seat and tried to catch it.

"Well, nothing's broken at least," said Grandma Luck as the turkey landed with a thud.

"It looks kind of nice in those yellow flowers," said Grandma McGuire.

Ma looked at Dad and started to giggle.

"So sorry," he said.

"Never mind," she said. "We'll just brush it off."

The turkey was put on its platter again. Dad carved it and then we all ate. And ate. First I was the stuffing hog, then I went to manicotti. I made sure I was a greens hog, since greens are my favorite. By the time I got to the sweet potatoes, I didn't feel much like pigging out anymore.

"I'm full as a tick," said Satch.

"I'm full as an elephant," said Jerry Lee.

"I'm so full, I can't say what I feel like," I said.

Grandpa Luck smiled at Ma and Dad. "Nice Thanksgiving," he said, "everybody together."

The telephone rang. Since Dad was sitting nearest to the kitchen, Ma asked him to answer it.

"It's someone named Jim," he called out from the kitchen.

I put my fork down. "Why is he calling?" I asked.

"I'll see," Ma said, getting up for the telephone.

A few minutes later my parents came in again.

"Jim just wanted to wish everyone a happy Thanksgiving," she answered.

"Well, I don't wish him one," I muttered.

"He's coming over before we head down to the Center," Ma said, ignoring me.

I slammed my elbows on the table. "How come he has to come over here? He just wants to spoil our Thanksgiving."

Ma cocked her head and gave me a warning look. "Jim is coming to help us cart the canned goods down to the Center." Down in our basement were boxes and boxes of food that Ma had collected for the community food drive.

"We can carry that stuff ourselves," I said. "Dad can help us."

"I think we can also use Jim's help," Ma said firmly, "and since he offered—"

Dad leaned over with a smile. "Who is this Jim guy?"

"A lousy old drug dealer," I blurted out.

Satch's eyes got wide. Ma's mouth dropped open and Grandpa Luck dropped his fork.

"That can't be true," said Grandma McGuire.

"Of course it isn't," Ma said. She glared at me. "Take that back, young lady."

"Why should I?" I blustered. "Ever since Dad has come back, Jim hasn't been around much. But before that he was hanging around all the time. And a friend of mine does think he's a drug dealer. He gets money envelopes and picks up weird people in his car. He wears big gangster hats and—"

Ma stood up. "Another word and you'll leave the table."

I shut up and she sat back down again. Dad took a deep breath.

Grandma Luck went to the sideboard. "How about some pie, everybody?"

"Pass it on," said Grandpa Luck.

"I'll be the pie hog," said Jerry Lee.

"No, I'm the pie hog," said Satch.

"Why doesn't one of you be the apple-pie hog and the other be the pumpkin-pie hog?" Grandma McGuire suggested.

Things settled down and we started to eat again. That is, until Dad stood up and tapped his fork on his glass.

"Attention, everyone," he said, "I have an announcement to make."

I kicked Satch under the table. This was it!

"First of all, I've got a new job," he said.

"Fantastic!" I yelled.

Ma beamed. "That's wonderful!"

"Hear! Hear!" said Grandpa Luck, clinking his own glass.

Dad was sitting next to Satch. "What kind of job is it?" Satch asked.

"A teaching job," Dad said. "I'll be teaching writing."

"About time!" Grandma Luck said in a jolly voice.

"I couldn't be more pleased," said Grandma McGuire.

"Where is the job?" Ma asked.

Dad rapped his fingers on the table. "That's the good part," he said. "I'll be working at a small school in Vermont. I think this family could use a change. And I've decided that we're all going to live there."

"Great!" I cried. "I knew you guys would get back together again!"

I looked at Ma. Her eyelids were fluttering.

"I've got a place for us to live," Dad pushed ahead, "—an old chicken farm."

"A chicken farm?" said Grandma McGuire.

"With real chickens?" said Grandma Luck.

"I like chickens," said Jerry Lee.

"Bravo," said Grandpa Luck. "I was wondering when you two would work things out."

Ma twisted her napkin. "But we haven't—"

"Uh-oh," said Satch.

"This is the first I've heard of a chicken farm in Vermont," Ma said. She looked at Dad and rapped her fingers on the table.

125

Dad smiled. "I thought I'd surprise you."

"You surprised me, all right," Ma said. "Though I'd say that *shock* is a better word."

"It sounds great to me," I said. "I think we should go. Don't you, Ma?"

"Things are not that simple, sweetheart."

"They're simple to me," I said. My voice was shaking. "Dad and you have been getting along fine."

"That's because we're not actually living together now. Things are complicated. I have a job here—"

I didn't let her finish. "We should have known that you would say no. That you wouldn't want to leave your precious Center and all your friends like Jim Signet."

"Nothing's been decided yet," Dad interrupted.

"Yes it has!" I cried. "Ma has decided. I can tell by the way she looks. She's going to say no, because she's selfish. She cares more about other people than she does us!" I stood up at the table. I was breathing hard.

"I have been busy—" Ma said, standing up too.

"Too busy," I said.

"You're upset," Ma said, reaching out to me.

"You're darned right I'm upset! This is my family, too, you know." I looked around the table. My grandparents looked sad. Jerry Lee and Satch were quiet.

My father had tears in his eyes. I was crying too. Crying hard. The one thing I'd been thankful for was all of us being together for once. But now I was losing it.

∮∮∮ 13 ∮∮∮

WE NEVER made it to the wishbone. Dad and Ma locked themselves in the downstairs bedroom to talk, while my three grandparents put away the leftovers. Any minute we were all supposed to drive down to Ma's Community Center with the boxes of canned food. We were supposed to help Ma pass out Thanksgiving dinners. Meanwhile, she and Dad were deciding what was going to happen to Satch and Jerry Lee and me for the rest of our lives.

"I like chickens," Jerry Lee said, waddling up to me. He had cranberry sauce next to his eyelid. "Listen . . . cock-a-doodle-do!" He flapped his arms like a rooster.

I wiped the cranberry sauce off his face. The huge dinner I had eaten felt like a big lump in my stomach. *Poor little guy,* I thought. *He doesn't know that his parents are in there, deciding his whole fate for him.*

Satch came over. "I told you they weren't going to get back together," he said.

"Nothing is decided yet, Mr. Smarty-pants," I said.

He pulled out his new tooth and stuck it back in again. "Don't forget, we've got a bet," he said.

I marched over to Ma's bedroom. I couldn't stand it anymore. "Can I come in, please?" I called loudly.

"Shh," said Grandma Luck. "They're having a serious discussion in there."

I leaned against the door. "Why can't I be a part of it?"

"They'll be out in a minute," Grandma McGuire said, tugging my hand gently.

The bedroom door opened a bit. Ma stuck out her face. Now it looked as if she had been crying. "Get ready to go to the Center, everybody."

"What did you decide?" Satch asked, jumping up. "Are we going to the chicken farm?"

Ma let out a sigh and turned back toward the bedroom. "See what you've done—"

"I thought you'd be happy," I heard Dad say. "I thought that everybody—"

"How could you?" Ma said, with her voice rising.

"It was just an idea—" said Dad.

I put my fingers in my ears. Their voices reminded me of how it used to be when Dad lived with us. My parents could never seem to agree. Ma liked the city and Dad liked the country. Ma wanted to spend all her free time with other people. Dad liked to be by himself writing his book. And then, when Dad's job fell through . . .

Suddenly, Jerry Lee was in front of my face, mouthing something. I took my fingers out of my ears.

"Can't we live in Washington, D.C., and Vermont at the same time?" he asked. "Can't we live in both places? In Washington I can go to kindergarten and then on Saturdays I could go to the chicken farm. I like chickens. Cock-a-doodle-do!"

I got up and ran to the front porch—just in time to see Jim's car pull up! I slammed the front door and faced him.

"I know you're trying to break my parents up," I said as Jim marched up the stairs. "But it's not going to work. My father and mother are getting back together."

Jim blinked. "Where's the canned goods?" He reached for the doorknob.

"We don't need your help," I said, barring his way.

His eyebrows knitted.

I flapped my arms in his face. "I thought you were scared of birds," I said. "Go on—get out of here! *Go away!*" I squeaked, imitating Rasputin. "We're moving to Vermont tonight. All of us—including my mother."

Jim's eyes narrowed. He was just staring at me. Ma came to the door. My whole family was standing behind her.

"Hi, Jim," she said. "Come in. The food's in the basement."

I dropped my arms and moved out of the way.

"What's all this I hear about you going north?" he said, passing by me.

I didn't hear Ma's reply. I did see through the door that she was introducing Dad to him. My father was actually shaking hands with the enemy.

Pretty soon, everyone was filing past me—Ma, Dad, Jim, my brothers and grandparents. And everyone was carrying something. I was freezing cold, but stuck to one spot. There were three cars going down to the Center, loaded up with canned goods and people. I waved good-bye to Grandma McGuire. She was sitting in the front seat of Ma's car. I was so afraid she'd ask me about the coin that I'd hardly spoken to her. Dad came up and put a hand on my shoulder.

"You don't look like you feel much like passing

out turkey wings. How about if I stay here with you?"

"You mean I don't have to go?" I let out a breath. I began shivering. I'd been standing outside for quite a while.

"There will be plenty of hands down at the Center," he said. "Why don't we walk off that dinner we put away?" He rubbed my back and I felt my shoulders relax.

"Okay," I said.

"Go get your coat," he said.

Dad gave Ma a nod and the cars pulled out. When I went to get my coat, my hands were shaking.

"Maybe we should let you warm up first," he said, when I got back. He fastened my top button.

"I'll be okay once we get going," I told him. "I don't want to go back inside for a while."

We walked down the back alley.

"Don't suppose you want to stop at the ice cream parlor?" he joked.

"Not really," I said. I turned to look at his face. I couldn't see his eyes because his glasses were fogged up.

"So, how did it go in there?" I asked.

"Not the way I'd hoped for. We're not going to work things out this time."

A big lump rose in my throat. "I thought so."

Dad sighed. "My plan has a few holes in it, I'm afraid."

"No, it doesn't," I said, grabbing his hand. "If only Ma would have listened."

He stopped. "She did listen. My plan wasn't great. I knew she wouldn't go for it."

"What are you talking about?" I said.

"I haven't even seen that chicken farm," Dad admitted. "The new job starts in a couple of weeks."

"So what?" I said. "That gives us time to pack our things."

"Your mother's got a job here, and her family. She can't drop everything."

"But you're my father!" I cried.

Dad took his glasses off. "Your ma and I really like each other. But we knew a long time ago that we were different."

"Then why did you get married and have kids?" I said, walking away from him.

Dad caught me. "We're different, but we loved each other. But now . . . we just can't work things out. Like I said, I knew she wouldn't go for it."

"Then why did you tell me it was such a good plan?" I said. "Why did you tell me that we'd be together?"

133

"Because I didn't want you to think that I didn't care," he said. "I wanted you to know that I tried."

"Well, you didn't try very hard!" I exploded. "Why did you think of a plan that you knew wouldn't work? You probably didn't want us to come to Vermont in the first place!"

"I do want you to come!" he exclaimed. "You can come without your mother, if you want to."

"I can?" I said.

Dad shuffled his feet. "Sure you can. As soon as I settle down and check the place out." He gave me a weak smile. "I told your ma that there weren't any real chickens still living on the farm. She hates chickens, you know."

I turned and faced my father. "Tell the truth, Dad. If you wanted things to work out, you would have figured out another place for us to live. You would have talked to Ma about it before today. You wouldn't have just sprung it on her."

"Guess I flopped again," Dad said. "But I meant well." He took my hands. "Try to understand. This job is important. In Vermont I'll have some peace and quiet. Maybe I can start on my book again."

"You and your stupid book!" I began to walk toward the house. "Books aren't more important than people. Ma is right. You have a big reality problem! You even killed our red Rabbit! You'll probably be glad if Ma marries Jim Signet. That's how much you care about us."

We were walking fast. Dad brushed my shoulder. "Jim's not a drug dealer," he said.

I looked straight ahead. "How would you know?"

"Because I know your mother," he said.

"I don't think so," I told him. "Otherwise, you'd figure out a way to get back together with her."

We were standing outside the front porch. Dad reached for me.

"I guess we're not the perfect parents."

"You're right about that," I said.

He motioned to the stairs. "Come on in. I'll make you some hot chocolate."

"No, thanks."

I turned away from him and crossed the street. I headed straight for Connie's. When I knocked on the door, she peeked and ran out. This time she had on her coat. I looked at her and cracked my knuckles, then held my breath for a minute.

"What's the matter?" she whispered.

I fought back my tears. "My dad and mom," I said.

"They're not getting back together?" she asked.

I shook my head.

"I'm sorry," she said. "When my mom and dad broke up, I was too little to think about it."

I looked across the street. Dad was still standing outside.

"I don't want to go home," I said. "Could we have a sleep-over?"

"I'm having a sleep-over at Anna's," said Connie. "My mother is taking me later. We're sleeping on the floor, on futons!"

"Oh."

She touched my arm. "Did you find your good luck?"

I looked across the street and Dad was gone. "I don't think I'll find it," I said. I wiped my nose with the back of my hand. Connie reached into her pocket and gave me a tissue.

"Most of the people I know have divorced parents," she told me.

I blew my nose. "I know. I was stupid to hope we'd be different."

I didn't go back to our house that day. I went over to my grandparents' and sat in their bedroom. I turned on the football game, then turned it off. The house was still. Even Rasputin was quiet. I leafed through a book in my grandmother's knitting basket. It was a play called *Raisin in the Sun* and was all about a family. I didn't feel like reading about families, so I stared out of the window. When Grandma and Grandpa Luck came home, they were surprised to see me.

"Can I spend the night here?" I asked. I had settled down on their bed and was clutching the edge of Grandma Luck's blue knitted blanket.

"If it's okay with your ma," said my grandmother.

"Will you call her?"

"I'll speak with her," Grandpa Luck promised, rubbing my head.

"You should have been at the Center," said Grandma Luck, kicking off her shoes. "I never saw so many turkey dinners. And the canned food drive was a great success—thanks to your mother."

"Please don't talk about my parents," I said.

"They still love you," she said, scrambling into her slippers.

I got up. "Excuse me," I said. "I'm going to my room."

In a few minutes Satch arrived with my pajama bag.

"The toothbrush is in the bottom," he said.

I dumped the bag out.

"You're not going to bed, are you? It's only seven."

"Maybe I will, maybe I won't," I said, shaking out my pajamas.

Satch sat on the edge of the bed. "I guess you heard they decided. They're definitely not getting back together."

"I guess you want your five dollars," I told him.

He screwed up his mouth and looked at the floor. He blinked and rubbed one of his eyes. "Keep it," he said. "Who needs five dollars?"

14

AFTER THAT my mind was a blank. At least I tried to make it a blank. I didn't want to think about my parents anymore. Not only were they not perfect, they were stupid.

After Thanksgiving vacation, when we got back to school, I met Arthur Cheever at his locker. "Okay, give it back," I said.

Cheever had a cold. He coughed in my face. "Give you what?" he hacked.

"Cover your mouth," I said. "The gold piece. You're the one who asked about cashing it in. I must have left it in my desk. Now it's not there."

Arthur snorted. "You think I stole it?"

"It's not worth five thousand dollars," I said. "So hand it over."

He pulled his pockets inside out. "Check it out. I don't have it."

I saw Joey Reid peeking around the corner.

139

Maybe he had stolen my good-luck piece. After all, he did hate me. But Joey wasn't even in our class. How could he have even known about the coin? I looked at him. He was still staring. "Is your friend a moron?" I asked Arthur.

Cheever glanced at Reid and chuckled. "Maybe he likes you," he said, leaning into his locker.

I felt the back of my neck get hot. "Why would he like me?" I said.

Arthur's face got kind of red. "Lots of people could like you," he mumbled. He looked at me. "You're very smart, you know."

I gulped. Maybe Satch was right. Maybe Arthur did like me. If he did, it would really be embarrassing because I didn't like boys. Especially boys who have pointy heads.

"You think I'm smart?" I couldn't help saying.

"Yeah," he said. He smirked. "Smart for a turkey."

"You're smart too," I said, pushing in front of him, "for a rodent."

It was hard to pay attention to Mrs. Jackson that day. I kept feeling inside my desk. I kept hoping the coin would turn up in some corner. I kept hoping that my life would get better.

But every day it rained. So there was no Explorers Club. Every morning Satch and I walked to school together. Every morning I watched out for Joey Reid.

Since that day in the doughnut store he hadn't bothered us. But I kept a lookout.

After school Satch and I walked home together too. We had to share an umbrella. Sometimes Connie walked with us because she was going to her grandmother's. On the days when we were alone, Satch and I talked. Every time it was the same conversation.

"When is Dad leaving for Vermont?" Satch would ask.

I'd say something like "I don't know and I don't care."

"You care," Satch would say.

"No, I don't."

"You care," he would repeat.

"And you don't," I would say. "You're glad our family's going down the drain. Aren't you?"

"Are you going to Vermont too?" he'd sometimes ask.

"I haven't decided yet. It would be nice not to be stuck like glue to you, for a change."

That's the kind of stuff we would say to each other. Deep down I knew that Satch must not be happy either. But I was still angry that he had made that bet with me. I was angry that he had been right —that Ma and Dad were too different to live with each other.

141

One day the sun came out. It felt great to be without an umbrella and not to have my sneakers sopping wet.

"Yea!" Satch shouted, running out of the school. "Today we can go to Explorers Club!"

"Shh," I said, looking around. "Do you want the whole world to know?" I smiled at him. The sun was out and I was happy in spite of myself.

"Oh, right," he whispered. "It's a secret. Don't worry—I won't tell anybody."

As usual I waited for Connie. As usual she came out with Anna. Nowadays Anna was being nice for some reason. I think she felt sorry for me because I'd lost my good-luck coin.

"Want a rice ball?" she asked, opening her lunch sack. Anna's mother sent these big sticky rice things with seaweed wrapped around them to school for her every day. She sent fried fish and chopsticks.

"No, thanks," I said. "Don't you get tired of those things?"

"Don't you get tired of peanut butter and jelly?" she said, stuffing the food into her mouth.

We walked over to the church. "My grandmother says it's going to snow," said Connie.

"Fat chance," I said. I remembered the last big snow a couple of years back. How Satch and Dad and I had had a snowball fight. "It never snows anymore."

"I think it's going to snow tonight," Satch said. He licked his finger and stuck it into the air. "I predict it," he said.

The path to Topknot Cave was muddy. Almost all the trees were bare. "Pretty soon we'll have to stop coming here," said Connie, with her teeth chattering. "We'll have to find someplace warm to explore."

"I'm never going to stop coming here," I said. "Not even in winter. Who knows? Maybe I'll even live here."

"What would you eat?" Anna said. "Tree bark?"

"No," I said, "I'd find the giant's stash and live on candy bars."

Connie giggled. "I'd come for supper," she said.

I smiled. "You would?"

"If you're having candy bars," she answered.

"So would I," Satch said, leaping into the air.

"Hey, look," said Anna. She was bent over the ground. "Footprints!"

We ran to see. Someone's big sneaker had sunk into the mud.

"Here's another one," I said, walking ahead.

Connie gasped. She was a few feet in front of me. "Look at this! Blood!"

We scrambled along the path to see. There was a dark red blotch on a mound of leaves and a trickle of red on the earth.

143

"Maybe an animal got hurt," Connie said.

"Maybe somebody got murdered," said Anna.

Satch put his nose close to the ground and took a sniff. "This isn't blood," he said. "It's paint."

We walked on for a bit and came to another spot, a big splotch of orange in the middle of the path. Then we passed a tree with a big white spider spray-painted on it. "Who would be stupid enough to paint a tree?" I said.

We looked at each other. I knew the answer to my question as soon as I'd asked it.

We began running. My heart raced as we turned toward the cave. I drew in my breath. One whole side was painted orange!

"The Avengers," Anna said grimly.

"Must be," said Connie.

Suddenly we heard a loud shriek. "Let's get out of here!" I said, grabbing Satch's hand. But when we turned toward the woods, they jumped out at us. The group was all there, Dangerfield, Reid, Cheever, and String Bean. We scattered and began running in the opposite direction. Satch and Connie were both holding on to me.

"What a bunch of wimps," Luke Dangerfield said, coming after us and laughing.

"You're the wimps," Anna screamed, wheeling around. "You painted our cave! You had no right to!"

"Oh, yeah?" said Luke. As he approached, we began to back up.

"Th-this . . . is, uh, private property," Connie stammered, holding her ground for a minute.

Luke shoved her. "You're right. It belongs to the Avengers. Out of my way."

"Watch who you're pushing," Connie said.

"Yeah, watch who you're pushing!" I yelled.

Luke turned on me. I caught my breath. The pimples on his face were red and ugly.

"We found this cave first," I said. "It belongs to the Explorers. You're just messing it up."

"Says who?" Luke said. He picked up a can and aimed it. Blue paint rained out of the air. I ducked and covered my face with my arm.

"You want to be permanently blue?" Luke said.

"Leave my sister alone!" Satch shouted.

"Chill out," said Luke. "I ain't going to bother her. I got better things to do with my time."

"Oh, yeah?" said Anna. "Like what?"

"Like fix up my headquarters," Luke said with a snarl on his face. "From now on this is the Avengers' hangout. Forget the Explorers."

String Bean laughed. Arthur Cheever came forward.

"Maybe we should let them have the cave back," Arthur said nervously. "After all, they were—"

"They were nothing," Luke shouted. "Don't tell me what to do!"

Arthur backed up and sat on a rock. "Sorry," he said, hunching his shoulders. "Guess this cave belongs to the Avengers now."

Luke pointed up at something. "Hey, what's that?" he shouted.

"What's what?" Joey Reid answered, from the roof of the cave.

Luke kept pointing. "That little rock on top," he said. "You painted it purple."

"I put my mark on it," said Joey.

"Who gave you permission?" said Luke.

"Nobody."

Luke leapt up onto the roof. "You jerk! I'm the leader of the club."

"That should have been Luke's spot," String Bean said from the ground. "That little rock should have had a red scorpion on it. Not a purple roach."

"Sorry," Joey said, dropping his paint can.

"Sorry doesn't count, you little punk," Luke said, pushing him.

"Uh-oh," said String Bean, letting a laugh out, "you're going to get it, Reid."

Joey seemed to shrink in size. He backed up and stumbled. Luke grabbed him by the shirt. "You're always doing what you want to do. When will you learn that I'm the leader of the club? You stinking zebra!"

My chest tightened and I took a quick breath. I thought for a minute that Luke had called Satch or me "zebra." But it was Joey Reid he was talking to.

Anna gripped my arm.

"There's going to be a fight," whispered Connie.

"Let's get out of here while the getting's good," Anna said, backing up. Satch turned to me. His eyes were frightened.

"Let's go," Connie said, grabbing my arm. "What's wrong with you, anyway?"

I stood there. I watched Luke push Joey down to the ground. I watched him put a foot on his back. I heard Joey crying. I couldn't leave.

"Throw me the black paint!" Luke ordered String Bean. "We'll show this zebra a thing or two."

"Oh, my gosh," Anna breathed. "What's he doing?"

"Hey, man," Arthur piped up. "Reid didn't mean anything—"

"Throw me the white too!" Luke shouted over him.

Two cans of spray-paint flew up to the roof. Luke still had Joey pinned with his foot. He caught the black paint. The can of white hit the ground. He aimed the can of black at Joey's back.

147

"Hey, man," Joey whimpered, "what are you going to do with that?" He struggled to stand up, but Luke pushed him down again. He pressed the button on the can and a stream of black paint flew out. The back of Joey's jacket was covered with a big stripe.

String Bean howled. "Now he really looks like a zebra."

I could hear Connie breathing hard, next to me. Anna and Arthur were backing away into the trees. Satch was holding real tight to my hand. My mouth was dry and I could hear my heart pounding. I still couldn't move.

Luke sprayed Joey's back with the other can. Joey screamed as if he were hurt.

"Now you got two stripes," he said, "a white and a black one!" Joey curled up in a ball and began sobbing. With a can in each hand Luke took aim again.

"Stop it!" I cried, jerking away from Satch. I felt my legs moving. I climbed up onto the roof.

"You want your stripes too?" Luke said to me.

I clenched my fists and swallowed. "Leave him alone," I said. "Leave him alone or I'll tell the whole world what you've done!"

"Yeah!" Anna called out from the trees. "We're getting the cops on you!"

"You want to go to jail?" screamed Connie. Luke

dropped his arms and I stepped in front of Joey. His hair and jacket were soaked and he was covering his face with his arm.

"That paint can blind or suffocate him," I told Luke. "There are a lot of witnesses here."

"She's right, man," Arthur said, coming out of the woods. "Messing up rocks is one thing. We can't mess up a person. Let Reid alone."

Luke looked around. He was outnumbered. Even String Bean had stopped laughing. He let his paint cans fall to the ground.

"Get up," he said, poking Joey with his foot. Joey stood up slowly. He was still crying and covering his face. He jumped off the rock and streaked through the woods. I felt my knees buckle.

I don't remember how I got down off the cave roof. I just remember grabbing Satch by the hand and running.

We ran like wildfire—Connie, Anna, Satch, and me. We ran to Pitts Place without stopping. Connie was crying and wiping her nose on the sleeve of her jacket.

"That was the meanest, yuckiest thing I ever saw in my life," Anna said hoarsely. She moved around in one spot, stamping her feet on the ground. "Those Avengers are disgusting."

"Do you think they'll come after us?" I said.

"We just have to stay away from them," Connie sniveled. "We can't ever go up there again."

A tear fell out of my eye. I was shivering. Satch was standing next to me, all hunched over. I could hear his teeth chattering.

Suddenly, Anna reached for me. "You did good," she said, giving me a quick hug. "You're okay, Daughter."

"Thanks," I said in surprise.

"Let's go," Connie said, yanking Anna by the sleeve. The five of us glanced back up the hill toward the woods.

"Right," I said, feeling for Satch's hand, "we'd better go home and lay low for a while."

Anna touched my shoulder. "Are we going to tell?"

"I don't know," I said, hurrying away. "We'll talk about it later."

Anna and Connie went their way and Satch and I went ours. My brother and I started to run again. In a minute or two I heard Satch crying.

"I'm sorry," I heard him say at my elbow.

"Me too," I said. "It's rotten."

"It was my fault," he shouted into the wind.

I slowed up. "What do you mean?" I asked.

His head slumped. "I told them," Satch confessed.

"I told Arthur Cheever about Topknot. If it hadn't been for me—"

"You traitor!" I exploded. "Now everything's ruined. It was supposed to be a secret."

"I know," he said, grabbing my arm. "I didn't think that— It was only Arthur I told and—"

"Leave me alone!" I said, snatching my arm away. "Get lost! Go home by yourself."

"I'm sorry," Satch whined, following after me.

"Didn't you hear me?" I screamed, running as fast as I could. "Get away from me! You're not my brother anymore!"

"But Ma said—" He stopped and stood in one spot.

"I don't care what Ma says," I shouted, flying down the hill. "I don't care about anything anymore! Especially about what happens to you!"

⅋⅋⅋ 15 ⅋⅋⅋

I WAS almost at home when Arthur caught up with me. When I heard the footsteps racing behind me, I thought it was Satch. But then somebody pushed me on the back of the shoulder and Cheever was standing there. "Your little brother got hit," he said.

I jerked. Arthur's whole face looked pointy. His ears were sticking out from his cap and the tip of his nose was red from the cold, and dripping. His eyebrows were arched up. "Your brother got hit by a car," he said, catching his breath.

"You liar!" I said. "Haven't you and your friends done enough for one day?"

"It's true!" he yelled as I began running again.

"And you're sick!" I yelled back.

But Grandma Luck was standing on the front porch when I got there. She was wringing her hands and Jerry Lee was crying. She hugged me. "We thought you might be with the ambulance," she said.

My throat closed. "What ambulance?"

"Your ma has gone to the hospital. . . ."

I jumped down the steps.

"Come back!" she shouted. "Where are you going?"

I ran across the street without looking back. It was like a bad joke. I'd seen Satch not ten minutes ago. How could he have been run over by a car in that time? It couldn't be true. . . .

I took off up the alley. I passed Pitts Place again. I headed up Morris. I ran until my legs ached. All the way up the hill to Newton Elementary.

The street was empty. Satch was nowhere. In fact there was no sign of anything. I listened hard. No sound of an ambulance. The sky was getting dark. I pinched my cheek really hard. Maybe I was asleep and about to wake up, I thought. I remembered my grandmother's face on the porch and started shaking inside. "We thought you might be with the ambulance," she had said. I heard Arthur Cheever's voice: "Your little brother got hit. . . ." This whole day had to be a bad dream!

But when I went across the street, the painted white spider was still on the tree. And the topknot on

Topknot Cave was wet purple. And the mouth was red and the side was orange. And the earth was streaked with black and white paint and blue specks. The day had happened, all right.

A twig snapped in the woods. I turned around. It was nobody. I wondered if Joey Reid had paint in his eyes. I wondered how Satch was in the hospital. . . .

I sat down at the edge of the cave. I couldn't go home. I watched the sunlight drain from the sky. If Satch was hurt badly, it was my fault. What difference did it make that Satch had told Arthur Cheever about Topknot? Ma had told me to watch out for him. And instead I had left him. I had told him I didn't care what happened to him. But I did care what happened. I cared so much! I thought, beginning to cry.

Suddenly, a big pile of feathers swirled in front of my eyes. Eerie white in the dusk—it was snowing. I crept into the cave a little farther. I wasn't frightened. The palm of my hand struck something hard. I felt for it in the dark. Something smooth and round was just beneath the surface. I scratched around in the dirt and picked it up. I rubbed it and blew on it. It was my good luck. I'd lost it in the cave somehow, and now I'd found it. I put the coin in my pocket and turned to the door.

The giant was there.

"What do you want?" I said, scooting into the belly of the cave.

The tall, fat man leaned in closer. "I'm not going to hurt you," he said, reaching for me.

I kicked his hand and screamed. I lunged into the dark, clawing my way to the back opening. The moon was right in front of me. Pushing myself out, I gasped for air. I jumped to my feet.

But someone else grabbed me.

It hadn't been the moon in my face at all, but a flashlight. And the person holding my arm was Jim Signet.

"Got you, you little squirrel!" he said. I tried to jerk my arm away. "Thought you could lose us, eh?"

"What do you want?" I cried.

Jim's hand relaxed. "To take you home," he said.

I looked up at his face. Snow was on his eyebrows. He wasn't wearing his hat. "Your mother and father are going crazy," he told me. "Hey, Peanut," he called, "I got her!"

The giant lumbered around the corner, rubbing one of his hands.

"This is my friend Peanut," said Jim. "Your mother's met him, too, down at the Center."

The big man nodded. "Sorry to scare you," he said gently. "I've seen you up here sometimes."

"I'm sorry I kicked your hand," I said.

"Let's go," Jim said.

"What about Satch?" I asked.

Jim brushed some snow off my back. "Satch is copacetic," he said. "He's a tough little squirrel."

My heart raced ahead of my feet as we hurried toward Pitts Place. Satch was okay! When we got to the street, Ma and Dad were coming up the hill from the opposite direction. They were holding hands and Ma had her green coat on. Leaving Jim behind, I ran toward them. I slid and almost knocked Dad to the ground. Ma caught me.

"Is Satch really all right?" I breathed into her coat.

"He's fine, honey. The car braked before it hit him. He fell and bumped his head. I think he was shocked more than anything."

Dad had his arms around me. "Don't you ever run away like this again." His eyes were full of tears. "Satch told us about the incident at the cave. We love you, sweetheart."

I began to blubber like a baby. "I'm sorry I let Satch go home by himself."

Dad hugged me harder.

"Let's go," said Ma.

Jim and Peanut gave us a ride. As soon as I got home, I ran upstairs. Satch's eyes were closed and he had a big bandage on his head. Grandpa Luck was sitting next to him, holding his accordion.

"Is he asleep?" I whispered.

Grandpa nodded. "I think so. The doctor said he was fine. But I'm keeping him company."

I motioned to Grandpa. "I'll do it for a while."

My grandfather got up slowly. He put down his accordion and walked away. "Don't mind telling you, we were scared when that call came in," he said. "Then when we heard about that awful stuff happening on the church grounds . . . and you disappearing . . ."

"I shouldn't have run away," I said. "I shouldn't have worried you."

"All's well that ends well." He sighed.

As soon as he left the room, Satch opened his eyes.

"Did I wake you up?" I asked.

"I'm not sure I was sleeping," said Satch. "I think I was just playing possum."

I peered at the patch on his forehead. "Does your head ache?"

"No, I just have a goose egg. It was bleeding a little. That's why I've got the bandage on."

"Was the ambulance scary?" I asked, sitting on his bed.

Satch sat up a little. "No, it was fun."

"I'm sorry for what I did," I said, taking his hand. "I shouldn't have let you go home by yourself."

"I'm sorry too," said Satch. "I shouldn't have told Arthur Cheever about your cave."

"That's okay," I said. "The Avengers might have found it anyway. Just like the Explorers did."

"I always hated Luke Dangerfield," said Satch. "But Arthur Cheever is funny. He was teaching me how to draw things on the playground."

"It's okay," I said. "Really."

I propped his pillow up. "Would you like some juice?"

"Grandma Luck gave me enough soup for supper to sink a boat," he said, giving me a big grin.

I looked at his mouth and winced. "What happened to your new tooth?" I asked.

"It cracked in the accident. Ma says the dentist can get me another one," Satch said. "Guess it's better to be a snaggletooth again than to get your neck broken." He laughed and showed the space in his mouth. I patted his foot.

"I'm sure glad that you're okay," I said.

Satch leaned forward and looked straight at me. "You were brave," he said.

"I was?"

"I would have been too chicken to stop Luke Dangerfield," he said. "If it hadn't been for you, Joey Reid wouldn't have gotten away. Who knows what Luke would have done to him?"

"I sure wouldn't have wanted that to happen to you or me," I said.

"But you hate Joey," said Satch. "What made you stick up for him?"

"I don't know. I just did it, that's all." I tweaked his toe. "I have something for you." I reached into my pocket and held out the coin.

"Your good-luck piece," said Satch. "You found it."

"Take it," I said, handing the coin over.

Satch looked puzzled. "But it's yours."

"It belongs to all of us," I said. "I kept it for a while. Now it's your turn."

Satch's whole face lit up. He touched the coin with his finger. "I'll take good care of it," he said.

I turned to leave. "Guess I'll let you get back to playing possum for a while."

"Wait a minute," he said. "Just one thing . . ."

"What is it?" I asked.

"I'm always going to be your brother. There's no way you can change that, no matter what happens."

"I don't want to change it," I said.

"Are you going to Vermont with Dad?" he asked.

I giggled. "I think I've 'chickened' out of that idea."

Satch laughed. Ma and Dad came into the room. Jerry Lee came, too, holding tight to his teddy bear.

159

"How's our number-one guy?" Dad asked Satch.

Satch stuck his thumb up.

"Before you go to sleep," Ma said, "we have an announcement to make." She looked at us three kids, then at my father. Dad nodded.

"We're going to try again," she said.

I couldn't get what she was telling us, at first. But Satch caught on right away.

"You're staying married?" he exclaimed.

Dad chuckled. "Something like that."

"We're going to be under one roof again," said Ma, "as soon as possible."

"Isn't that something?" said Jerry Lee.

I grinned. "That's something, all right." I turned to my parents. "I thought you said you were too different."

"We're different," Ma admitted, "but not too different to know that we still love each other."

"Not too different to work harder at being a family," said Dad. "Besides," he added, "differences can be very exciting." My parents smiled at each other and shook hands.

16

WHEN A notice was sent home asking for information about the "incident," Satch and I had a talk with Ma and Dad. Then we all went with Connie and Anna and their parents and spoke with the principal. Mrs. Jackson came, too, and so did Arthur Cheever and his parents. Joey Reid's dad had reported what had happened to his son. I guess what Anna had said about Joey's dad being in jail wasn't true. When Mrs. Ham, the principal, asked us what had happened, we just told things the way we had seen them. The principal said thanks and a few days later Luke Dangerfield wasn't in school anymore and neither was String Bean. I think that they were suspended. Dad said that Satch and I had done the right thing by talking. That people who do things like spray other people with black and white paint shouldn't get away with it. People who paint other people's property get in trouble too. Like Arthur Cheever. He has to work on the church grounds, picking up litter, to make up for the damage he did. Arthur was the one who had painted the white spider on the tree.

I'm not sure how Joey fits into all the punishment stuff. After all, he did graffiti on the church grounds too. But I don't think anyone was interested in punishing him much, after what had happened to him. From that day on Joey was different. I saw him on the way to school sometimes, but he never threw rocks at me. He never called me names either. I still can't figure out why he had called me and Satch "zebra," when it turned out that he was just like us. Well, like us in that he's of different races. That's the only way that Joey is like me and Satch, as far as I know, though. I guess we really don't know who he is, as a person. However, one day he did come up to us at the pickle store on Martin Luther King Avenue. Satch and I were at the counter buying two big ones. Joey was outside, with his nose pressed against the glass. And he was staring at us, just like in the old days.

"Here comes trouble," I said as he walked through the door. "Let's go."

"Just a minute," said Satch. He was trying to fit his pickle into his lunch box. I reached over and jammed it against his orange, then slammed the box quickly.

"Now my orange will taste like pickles," he said. "Thanks a lot."

By that time Joey was standing right next to us. I hurried to the door.

"Wait up," he said, following us.

Satch stopped and waited.

"Come on," I said, yanking my brother.

Joey got in front of me. "I just wanted to say . . . sorry for the other times," he muttered, staring at the ground.

"Forget it," I said, brushing past.

He touched my coat. "And thanks," he said. "Thanks for, you know . . . saving me."

At that moment he looked very ordinary. Not like a bully or even a wimp. He'd had a haircut and I could see his eyes. They were sad, like a hound dog's eyes.

"Forget that too," I said. "It's not as if I beat Luke Dangerfield up."

"That would be the day!" Satch said.

Joey smiled. "I don't think any of us would have the nerve to do that. But you did stand up to him."

I felt kind of proud when Joey said that. I had stood up to Luke. I'd done it without thinking. I wondered if I'd be that brave a second time. . . .

"Hey, Shorty," Anna said, ruffling Satch's hair. "What big teeth you have!"

Satch smiled. A couple of weeks after he'd broken the cap on his front tooth, Ma had taken him to the dentist to get him another one. He made a clicking sound with his teeth. "The better to eat you with, my dear," he joked with Anna. "Especially if you keep calling me Shorty like that."

"Sorry," she said.

The four of us linked arms and began walking. "Where are we going?" asked Connie.

"To the house where Frederick Douglass used to live," I answered. "It's just down the alley from where I live."

"I love that place," said Connie.

"Is it old and spooky?" asked Anna.

"It's not all that spooky," I replied, "but it is old." She curled her lip.

"Come on," I said, giving her arm a pull. "You'll like it."

"If you say so," she said. She smiled at me and I smiled back. The four of us swayed in a ragged line down the street.

"Next Saturday," Satch announced, "we're all going to a party."

"What kind of party?" Connie asked.

"For Jim Signet's business," I answered. "He's having a grand opening."

"Humph," said Anna. "What kind of business did he open? A gambling place?"

"Not exactly," I said.

The following Saturday, Connie and Anna went with my family. All of us brought our own laundry. The boarded-up candy store, where Jim had met Peanut that night, had a new window. And a flashing sign over the door said KEEP CLEAN AT JIMMY'S.

"I'll be darned," said Anna as we climbed out of the car. "It's a laundry."

I giggled. "I was just as shocked as you are when I found out," I said. "Even after Jim found me at the cave, deep down I was still convinced he was a crook of some kind."

Jim greeted us at the door. He had on a maroon suit and his black hat. Peanut was there, too, passing balloons out.

"Congratulations," I said, shaking Jim's hand.

"Thanks a lot, sister squirrel," he replied. I dumped my laundry on the floor. "Grab a machine," Jim said with a grin. "It's on the house today. Then go pig out on popcorn and soda."

"Oink, oink," I said with a laugh. I lugged my laundry bag over to an empty washing machine.

"How come you didn't tell us in the first place that you were opening a Laundromat?" I asked Jim.

Jim shuffled. "I didn't know if it would work out," he said. "Peanut and I needed investors . . . from the neighborhood. You know . . . people to give me some bread."

"Bread?" I said.

"Money," he said, handing over the soap powder. I felt myself smiling. Jim's language was funny, but I guess his heart was in the right place. I even figured out why he wears a big gangster hat—to hide his bald spot! I suppose that things do have a way of working out. . . .

Ma and Jim are still friends, but they're not romantic. And even though Dad did go to Vermont for one semester, he's going to come back. Then we're all going to live together again. Maybe not on Cedar Street, but hopefully somewhere else in the neighborhood. I don't want to transfer from Lucy Fig Newton. I've gotten to like it there. . . .

I finished my family heritage project for Mrs. Jackson's class. Now I know what to *call* myself— Daughter McGuire. I can also say that I'm African-Italian-Irish-Jewish-Russian-American. It's a mouthful, but I like saying it. Especially since I know a little bit about some of my ancestors. But the main thing I'm going to concentrate on now is not what to call myself, but what I'm going to do. What I'm going to do in my life, that is. For one thing, I want to explore. Not just caves, but mountains. I want to go to faraway places and meet lots of people. As soon as I can, I'm going to Western Africa, Ireland, Russia, and Italy. I'm also going to Japan to sleep on a futon. Actually, I might get to sleep on a futon next week, since I'm sleeping at Anna's house. Come to think of it, I want to go everywhere! I might even go to the moon! . . .

No, take that back. I'll stick to this planet. After all, it's my world.

About the Author

SHARON DENNIS WYETH grew up in Washington, D.C., where she attended public schools. She graduated from Radcliffe College in Cambridge, Massachusetts. She has written many books for young readers, including the Pen Pals series, *Annie K.'s Theater,* and *Once-in-a-While Dad.* She lives in Montclair, New Jersey, with her husband, Sims, and daughter, Georgia.